YUBI

AND THE

GOOD DOG OF TANGIBAD

by **GEORGIA HUNTER**

Blue Crow Books

ISBN: 1481961004
ISBN 13: 9781481961004

Library of Congress Control Number: 2013900846
CreateSpace Independent Publishing Platform
North Charleston, South Carolina

∾ Contents ∾

∾ **The Memory of a Great Dog** ∾

❧ The Pup ❧

"**W**ild dogs!" the boy yelled. He dashed to the ship's railing and peered toward the craggy cliffs. At first he couldn't make out where they were, for their wailing echoed from the rock face and skipped across the water as the sails flapped and popped, eager to fill with wind. Then he spotted movement on the steep slope. A small, black and white collie was being pursued by a pack of hungry hounds. The pup's paws pounded down the path towards the sea with the pursuers gaining on him; saliva drooled off the tips of their tongues.

The boy gestured with his arms and yelled, "RUN! RUN!" Ill-fated, his heartening words were lost in the sea breeze and the tide pulled the ship away from the dock.

The stray sprinted to the harbor and darted onto the wharf. His pace was steady like the swinging of his ears, back and forth, in rhythm with the sway of his withers, but he was tiring. His followers sensed this. The leader let out a long, loud yowl and swiftly the pack spread out and circled the collie. They loped towards their prey with a bloodthirsty look in their eyes. He was trapped on the end of the pier.

Tobin, an old salty, rushed towards the boy.

"Yubi, what's happening?"

"It's the pup. The wild dogs have him cornered."

The collie, poised on the edge of the jetty, turned and faced the horde of marauders. Unblinking, he lowered into a crouching position, ready to fight for his life. His flews curled upwards exposing his strong white fangs and he snarled between deep breaths. Instinct told him he must not display weakness. The hounds hesitated, panting. Then, suddenly the leader leapt at the smaller dog, snapping and barking ferociously. The agile collie jumped sideways, catching the attacker's front paw in his jaw, crushing the bones and ripping the flesh. The leader drew back but the collie held on. The wild dog squealed and gnashed his teeth. This excited the others to attack. Instantly, the collie whirled around, releasing his hold on the leader who limped backwards, blood streaming from his wound. Just then a heavy-set dog with a brisket as wide as a pony, hurled himself into the fray, trying to bite the collie's throat. His wide chest struck the pup in the ribs and knocked him to the ground. The young, lean dog sprang up like a coiled cobra and, at the same time, kicked the monster with his strong hind legs and claws. All of a sudden two dogs attacked from the side, one sinking his teeth into the collie's withers and the second grasping his leg. The collie let out a mournful yelp and tried to pull away. He struggled to stay standing.

Yubi and Tobin yelled at the dogs from the deck of the *GOLDEN EEL*. They slapped their hands on the ship's railing and flapped their arms rowdily, but the dogs took no notice.

"Our hollering isn't going to help that pup," said Tobin, "Nothing can help him now. They'll have 'im torn to pieces in a few minutes."

Yubi glanced quickly at Tobin. "I have to do SOMETHING!"

"Nothin' can be done, lad."

Yubi was extremely agitated. "Something MUST be done." He ground his teeth and growled. He punched his fist into the sky.

Tobin jerked backwards.

Just then the collie and his attackers tumbled sideways and, for a moment, the pup disappeared under their large, furry bodies. They rolled over and over, screeching and snarling. Hair and blood flew every which way. Suddenly, the trio dropped off the edge of the dock and plunged into the water. All three vanished.

Yubi gasped.

"Heh!" blurted Tobin, pointing toward a head that bobbed on the surface. "Isn't that the pup?" He turned to face Yubi, but Yubi had climbed onto the bulwarks, ready to dive.

"Don't, Yubi, the ship is pulling away with the tide. You'll never be able to swim back!" His words were for naught for Yubi had already flung himself in the water.

Tobin ran towards the captain's cabin yelling, "The kid's overboard! The kid's gone over!"

"Darn, kid! Drop the dinghy! Drag the anchor!" said the scowling captain.

Yubi swam towards the pup as the wild dogs crawled onto the shore, shaking the water off their red-stained coats. As the gang slunk away, the lead dog raised his nose skyward and gave a long eerie cry.

The collie paddled aimlessly, struggling to stay afloat. His strength was spent; the water surrounding him was stained pink with his blood. When Yubi reached him, he clutched the hair on his neck to hold his head above water. He wrapped his arm around his body and pulled him close to his chest. He trod water, looking back over his shoulder towards the ship.

"Yubi, Yubi, hold on," called the sailors as their oars sliced rhythmically into the deep blue and the small boat came alongside the boy and the dog.

Quickly and quietly they returned to the main ship where the ship's doctor patched up the bloodied animal as well as he could.

"He's a mighty mess," he said, "Don't put too much hope on him surviving, Yubi."

Yubi crouched beside the pup, patting his head gently. He covered him with a piece of old canvas sail. The dog whimpered softly and closed his eyes.

Captain Pigalli's lips puckered and he shook his head from side to side. His tongue clucked in his mouth as he stared down his nose at the boy.

"Not a smart thing to do, Yubi. You put this ship at risk and all the men on board for a useless beast. What were you thinking; if you were thinking at all?"

Yubi cast his eyes downward.

"What have you got to say for yourself?"

"I'm . . . I'm sorry."

"Is that all?"

"I . . . I had to help the dog," Yubi said, feeling feeble.

"And jeopardize the *GOLDEN EEL*?"

Yubi attempted to explain, "The day that . . ."

"I'll hear no excuse. You have made an error in judgment. Now, be man enough to admit it."

Captain Pigalli's scolding stung like a slap on the cheek. Yubi felt ashamed.

∽ The Canary Islands ∽

Later, in his bed, Yubi could see with his eyes closed. The image was vivid and gave him a sour stomach. It was his father saying, "You can't come with me, you have to stay here." Then his father turned and walked away from him. That was two years earlier, when he was twelve. The recollection was as clear as if it happened yesterday but the separation felt like it had been a lifetime. He had never felt loneliness until that moment and now his body ached with it, inside and out, in his head and in his heart.

His father had felt the bite of loneliness too, since Yubi's mother had become ill and died.

Shortly after her death, he announced, "I have to make some money for us and you need to stay in the village and learn a trade."

"I don't want to, I want to be with you," pleaded Yubi.

"You can't. Besides, it's too dangerous to take you where I'm going."

"Please don't leave me," Yubi cried.

"Don't cry, son, I'll come back for you as quickly as I can. You can live with the mill keeper until I return in a few months."

And then, he hugged him good-bye.

But two years had passed since then. And once again, Yubi felt the strong pang of loneliness as he remembered seeing his father load pistols and cannons onto the ship and, later, sitting on the dock, watching until the ship disappeared from sight. All he knew was that his father sailed to the Canary Islands. Now tears welled up under his eyelids and pushed through at the corners, rolling silently down his cheeks. He sniffed and breathed deeply as he rubbed them away with the side of his hand. He thought about Captain Pigalli. When the captain had heard that Yubi's father had not returned he offered to help. "We're sailing to the Canary Islands, you can apprentice on the *GOLDEN EEL* after you finish your schooling."

They sailed to the Canary Islands a few months later and landed in Tenerife but there was little information about Yubi's father. Some of the sailors thought they had remembered his ship although it hadn't been seen or heard of for months. Yubi was heart-broken. He felt bereft of life.

One afternoon he left the *GOLDEN EEL* and climbed the steep mountain path that paralleled the seashore. It felt good to hike up the rough trail even though the muscles in his legs ached and he panted like a dog. When finally, he was too weary to go on, he sat on the edge of a jagged cliff looking back toward the city. He sucked the clean air up into his nostrils, filling his lungs to the brim. Unexpectedly, something nudged him between his arm and ribs.

"Where did you come from?" a surprised Yubi said as he looked into the brown eyes of a young dog. The dog wagged his tail and his head pressed into Yubi's side. He was black except for a white blaze on his face and long white hair tipping his tail.

The next morning Yubi went to the same spot on the steep path, hoping to find the pup again. He was there, waiting, and so he did each day after. The dog filled Yubi's heart with joy. In the late afternoon the pup would follow him to the edge of the village, stop and sniff the air, then retreat to the underbrush, peeking out to watch Yubi walk to the end of the pier and onto the *GOLDEN EEL*.

One day Yubi asked Captain Pigalli if the dog could come aboard.

"No animals, Yubi," was the captain's reply.

❧ Cochineal ❧

Yubi's sleep was jagged and filled with unsettling dreams. He woke earlier than usual. He rubbed the sleep away from his eyes with the knuckles of his index fingers and yawned lazily. The smell of steamy, sweet gruel cooking in the galley, as it did each morning, teased his nostrils. He pulled back the covers and thrust his feet out from under the blankets. His long legs dangled like lima beans above the dark floorboards as he gazed around the room. The space was small and shabby and it made him feel hemmed in, but it was his home thanks to Captain Pigalli. His finger and thumb plucked mechanically at the skin beneath his lower lip. Suddenly he remembered the dog!

He bounced to the upper deck to find the pup in the same place he had left him the night before. He leaned down to check the dog's wounds and soothe him. "You're looking better," he said as he patted the collie's head and gave him a hunk of salt pork.

While the dog chewed on the meat, Yubi stood alongside and peered across the blue-green sea. The Canary Islands had all but disappeared into the horizon except for the flat top of the huge volcano Teide. Then he caught a glimpse of something else. He half-closed his eyes to see more clearly. The dog lifted his head and whimpered, sensing a change in Yubi's mood. "Might be trouble!" Yubi said to the pup. The collie's ears perked up. Yubi shouted to the helmsman, "Ship aft!" He ran to Captain Pigalli. "There's a galleon astern."

"What's her flag?"

"I couldn't make it out."

Captain Pigalli sighed as a deep furrow wrinkled his brow. He stepped back from the chart he was studying, moved around the desk, and walked towards the door. He grabbed the looking glass off the shelf next to the door. "Let's hope she doesn't have a Jolly Roger."

Yubi felt his stomach somersault. "What would pirates want with US?"

"The cutthroats aren't interested in us, except, maybe, to have our livers for lunch! It's our cargo they're after."

"The cochineal? Why?"

"They'll sell it on the black market. It's as valuable as gold these days and the pirates know the textile merchants won't ask any questions if they can buy the crimson dye cheap."

Pigalli held the looking glass up to one eye and peered in the direction of the distant galleon. Yubi stared intently too. With the glass still to his eye, Pigalli said, "Looks like we're in luck, she's turning away."

Unexpectedly, the pup came alongside, which startled the two gazers. The collie raised himself onto his hind legs, leaning his front paws on the bulwarks. His eyes raked the horizon and he growled at the distant vessel.

"Well!" laughed the older man, "looks like you'll make a good merchant sailor after all!"

"Then . . . can . . . can he stay?" asked Yubi.

"He can stay, but he's your full responsibility. Any trouble, he's off."

From that moment Yubi and the dog were inseparable.

"What are you gonna' name him?" Tobin asked a few days later.

"Cole."

"Umm, good," Tobin replied warmly. "He's healing up real well. He'll be a beauty some day and we already know he's darn plucky."

Cole studied every move while Yubi performed his duties. He watched when the carpenter, Hack, showed Yubi how to check the hull for leaks, to fill the cracks with new oakum and to pound wood plugs into minute holes where necessary.

"Smart dog," the astonished carpenter said one morning when Cole brought him a fresh wood plug.

Cole stayed close when the Master Gunner taught Yubi to sift the gunpowder to keep it dry and to load a musket and a cannon. When Yubi studied the charts and learned to navigate, Cole sat beside him. If a ship passed, the pup ran to the railing, growling and barking.

"He's a smart fellow!" said Pigalli.

Yubi felt proud. Cole learned quickly. He would retrieve items on command. He learned the sailors by name too so that Yubi could say, *'Go fetch Tobin'* or *'Go fetch Hack'* and Cole would find them wherever they were on the ship.

Cole's favorite chore was swabbing the decks. He'd run and jump, biting at the water that flicked off the end of the mop.

∾ Davy Jones ∾

Early one morning Hack screeched. "Where's that DOG!"

"What's the matter?" said another sailor.

"He's stolen me slops!"

Tobin poked his head out from his bunk. "What's gotten into Hack?" he snuffled.

"The dog's stolen his clothes."

"Stolen?" Tobin croaked, still sleepy from the midnight watch he'd shared with Yubi.

"Yeah, I guess it's true 'cuz Hack has nothin' on, naked as a baby," the sailor chuckled.

"Where's he gone?"

"To the kid's quarters, I guess."

Tobin jumped out of his bunk.

"Well, get after him! You know what Hack is like when he gets an idea stuck in his head."

"Where's me slops, you drivelswigger?" yelled Hack as he swung open the door of Yubi's cabin with such force the leather hinge popped the nails from the casing.

"I . . . I . . . I don't know."

Hack's red face twisted and he brandished a rod, swinging it menacingly above his head.

Cole bounced to his feet, growling and baring his teeth.

"It's him who done it," Hack bawled and spun to face the collie.

"Done WHAT?" shouted Yubi.

"He took me slops!"

The rod sliced the air above Cole's head. Yubi burst forth and grabbed the dog just as the rod smacked the floor.

Hack raised his arm again.

"HACK!" bellowed Tobin, "DROP THAT ROD!"

"I ain't droppin' it 'til I get me duffle back. That beast took me things and now I ain't got no clothes."

"I can see that! You're standing in your birthday suit," said Tobin. He turned to the other sailor. "Get Hack some clothes and get Captain Pigalli."

A cluster of seamen gathered, gawking and snickering. Hack dropped the rod.

The sailor returned with some pants and a shirt, and the captain.

"The dog's a thief," Hack blabbered as he shoved one leg and then the other into the pants. "He's always sniffin' around. I see him snoopin' and now he's gone and stolen me things." He slipped the shirt over his head.

"What's this all about?" the captain said, turning to Yubi.

"I don't know."

"Look at those deadlights too!" Hack interrupted.

"Hold your tongue!"

"I ain't holdin' my tongue, the dog has the eyes of the devil."

Cole's eyes were locked into a piercing stare, unblinking and threatening.

"No dog gets the better of me," Hack taunted.

"I said hold your tongue or you'll be scrubbing with the holystone."

Hack was unrelenting. "I want me duffle."

"Get yourself up on deck — all of you," commanded Captain Pigalli. Then he turned to Tobin. "Get Hack a bar of sandstone and make sure he's scrubbing for three days. It'll give him time to cool down."

Tobin reached for the sailor's arm but Hack yanked it away and continued to eyeball the dog. "I'll see you to Davy Jones," he ranted. Then he grabbed the rod, which he dragged noisily over the floorboards as he stomped away.

"What does he mean, I'll see you to Davy Jones?" asked Yubi.

"It's a threat to get rid of your dog," Captain Pigalli replied.

Yubi gasped, "Would he REALLY do that?"

"Hack gets a thought into his head and can't let it go."

The captain gazed at the dog and then at Yubi. His index finger and thumb pinched his bottom lip, drawing the words out of his mouth. "I've seen Hack like this before. He had a row with a mate because of a parrot . . . accused him of undoing the latch on the birdcage . . . threatened him with Davy Jones. The sailor denied it, over and over. Hack wouldn't listen to reason.

Finally, the seaman got fed up, drew his cutlass and hacked off Hack's nose. Never saw the parrot or the end of his nose again."

Yubi gulped. "And so the nickname Hack?"

"That's right."

"Cole didn't take Hack's things. I'm sure of it. I would have known," an anxious Yubi blurted.

Captain Pigalli straightened his shoulders and jutted his chin. "Keep the dog in line. I have no time for problems with dogs or with Hack. Getting the cochineal to its destination is my only concern." He turned and walked away.

⤳ Macramé Knots ⤳

Hack was down on his knees scrubbing with the holystone. He looked like a monk in prayer, his baggy clothes mushrooming out from his bowed head. Once, when Yubi had to pass close to him, Hack gave Cole the evil eye. The dog sensed the man's anger and shifted his stance. Yubi felt a shivery ping between his shoulder blades, so he quickly led the dog to the farther end of the ship.

"I'll show you a trick!" he said.

Cole tweaked his head from side to side and pinned his attention on the rope that Yubi pulled from a box.

"This is a one-handed knot trick," said Yubi.

He draped the rope over the back of his hand, tilting it slightly. Then he hooked his small finger over one section of rope while reaching the other section of rope with his first and second fingers. Quickly, he let the rope slip off his hand and gave it a swift shake. Suddenly the rope was perfectly hitched. Cole moved toward it and sniffed at the knot.

"Cole better not get his nose too close when you do *that* trick," bellowed Tobin, "Might have to nickname him Knot!" He let out a huge belly laugh.

Yubi laughed too and Cole pranced in circles, holding his snout high in the air as if to say *you'll never get my nose!*

"Move over . . . I'll show you something," said Tobin. He pulled some ends of rope from the bin and crouched alongside Yubi and the dog.

His fingers deftly twined the ropes into knots. "Half knot tying is much easier if the center string is taut and secure, like this. The over hand knot is simple too and uses a single rope, like your trick. Fancy knots, the Picot and Lark's Head, are more for decoration. It's macramé."

"Can you teach me how to do it?"

"Sure."

Tobin demonstrated step by step, looping or twisting the cords into beautiful knots.

"How did you learn to do these?" Yubi asked.

Tobin mused, "Well . . . it was a long time ago. I was younger than you are when I told my mom I was going to sea. She didn't want me to, but I was a cocky kid. She cried. I boasted, *'I'll be back sooner than it takes for your tears to dry.'* But, I was very, very wrong. My dear mom was long-gone to heaven by the time I returned." Tobin stopped talking. He breathed deeply, which made a fizzing sound go up his nostrils. The dog stared, quizzically. For a moment, the old salty gazed at the horizon; his heavy eyelids drooped over moist eyes. "We were sailing to the coast of Africa, heading to Tangibad. One night our ship was damaged by a gale and we barely made it into port. She'd taken on a lot of water and it was obvious we were gonna' lose her. She went down like a lead weight, so fast none of the cargo could be saved. Within a week the captain booked passage on the next ship leaving Tangibad. So did some of the sailors. I asked the captain to lend me enough for a ticket. *'No cargo, no pay,'* he said. I pleaded not to be left behind. When the ship sailed away, I cried like a baby. A Moor, by the name of Abdul-Rahim, was watching and he took pity on me. His family had a factory that made colorful blankets, fringed with elaborate macramé, sometimes with beads interwoven. Abdul taught me how to do it. *'You can work in our factory and earn enough to return to your home,'* he offered. I was grateful, although it took me many months to earn enough. The day I was to leave, I cried again for, by then, Abdul was my best friend. I'll always remember his parting words to me . . .

> *'Separated,*
> *But not apart,*
> *Carried, forever,*
> *In each other's heart.'*

Abdul told me of one last knot before I left. *'This is a secret knot, used only to identify those closest to my family. If ever you come to Tangibad and I am not here, show this and any member of my family will welcome you.'*

"Many years *have* passed since then, yet, he is still here."

Tobin laid his hand on his heart. "Now, Yubi, I will teach the knot to you."

∽ **Mad Man** ∽

The next day, Hack's clothes were discovered under his mattress.

"Doddering old fool," said the cook as he spooned grey gruel into bowls.

"We ain't safe with a madman aboard," cut in a wart-faced sailor who was sitting at the far end of the table.

"Whacha gonna' do about it?" asked the cook.

"He won't do nothin' except, maybe, grow another wart," laughed a sailor.

Wartface didn't flinch.

"I'd sleep easier if the old fool just vanished," said the cook.

The warty sailor finished eating his gruel. Then he swaggered out of the galley, muttering under his breath, "I'll show them!" On the upper deck, he went to the far end of the ship, passing by Yubi, who was repairing a sail. Cole sniffed the air as he passed.

Later, Yubi said, "Come on, Cole, we need to sleep now so we can do the midnight watch with Tobin."

Cole paused, sniffed the air again, then bounced to Yubi's side and they went below deck.

Just after dark, the dog left the room. He followed a scent toward the end of the ship. He walked stealthily, ears perked, listening. Suddenly, he bound forward to the aft railing, barking.

"Shut that dog up!" someone yelled.

"Be quiet, Cole!" hollered another.

Cole kept barking, louder. He ran in circles.

"Stop that darn dog!" commanded a third.

Yubi stirred into consciousness. For a few seconds everything seemed a blur. He heard distant barking. "Cole?" he mumbled. "COLE! COLE!

Where are you?" Then he heard shouting and the thud, thud, thud of heavy footsteps running on the upper deck. The barking stopped.

Yubi jumped out of his bunk. He ran up the steps. His heart pounded in his chest as he charged towards the stern of the ship. He saw the silhouette of men leaning over the bulwarks. They were yelling at each other.

"Can you see him?"

"No!"

"He's over the side!"

Yubi rushed to the railing. "Is it . . . is it Cole?"

Just then a wet nose nuzzled into the palm of his hand. "Cole!" Yubi said relieved.

At the same moment, he realized there was a man over the side. The poor soul was dangling upside down. One foot was tangled in the rigging that draped over the railing. His body was limp, as if he was dead.

"Who is that?" Yubi asked.

"Hack!"

Men were shouting at each other.

"His boot is caught in the rigging."

"Don't yank on the rope, the boot may give way and the sea'll take him."

"Lower someone to get a hitch around him."

"Who's the lightest?"

"Yubi is!"

"Grab a rope! We'll lower you down."

"Tie him well, the wind is picking up," said Tobin, "Here, Yubi, take this and tie it around Hack's waist and over his shoulders, if you can."

Quickly the men harnessed Yubi with a safety rope. They held his arms as he slid one leg and then the other over the bulwarks. Unexpectedly, the ship rolled strongly to the port side. The sailors bellowed. Tobin hollered, "Hang on to him or he'll be smashed against the side." In spite of their best effort they lost their grip and Yubi swung away from the ship. Sailors screamed as the ship heeled to the other side. Yubi careened past. Tobin lurched forward, desperately grabbing for the safety rope. Cole ran pell-mell, his nails scratched across the planks as he struggled to stay standing. As Yubi swerved past for the third time, Tobin was able to seize the rope. "Are you alright, lad?"

"Yes!" he yelled back, "Now lower me down and be quick!"

Hand over hand, the men uncoiled lengths of rope until Yubi was hanging alongside the old seaman who moaned as Yubi hitched the rope around his body.

"Is he alive?" Tobin hollered.

"Yes! Pull us up!"

"Easy does it!" commanded Tobin, as the sailors' sinewy bodies tensed, ready to draw up the heavy weight.

Yubi clutched onto Hack, the galleon rolled to and fro and the men chanted, "One, two, heave. One, two, heave."

"Hurry up. Pull them in. I can't keep her steady much longer," called Captain Pigalli as he skillfully maneuvered the steering lever in the choppy sea.

Hack was crying when they laid him onto the deck. "I . . . I . . . I held on."

"Quiet, Hack," said Tobin, "You're bleeding badly, we have to get you bandaged."

"I . . . I . . . held on," he whimpered, "Because . . . Cole . . . was barking for me."

∾ Attacking Hack ∾

The next morning Captain Pigalli announced, "Hack needs to rest for a few days. Then he'll be as good as new."

"Thanks to the pup he's alive," said Tobin.

"That's for sure!" said one of the sailors.

"Yeah. You've got a great dog, Yubi."

A few days later Hack said, "I'm sorry, Yubi, for goin' after your dog like I did." His heavy-lidded eyes, like rumpled bed sheets, crinkled at the corners. "I forgot that I had put me slops under me mattress that day. I'm a forgetful old grouch, not good for much anymore. I don't even remember how I fell overboard."

After that, calm was restored upon the galleon until one afternoon Cole discovered Hack wandering aimlessly. "I'm lost," sobbed the old man when he saw the dog, "I can't find me home."

Suddenly a voice spouted from behind them, "What are you saying, you crazy old goat."

"I need to get home," whined frail Hack.

"The devil's got your mind," the intruder said threateningly. "We don't want a madman on this ship!"

"NO! NO!" pleaded Hack, "Don't push me over again!"

Cole jumped between Hack and his attacker and growled loudly. His lips curled into a snarl and he crouched, ready to spring. The assailant stopped dead in his tracks. His warty face contorted into a nervous frown. Then he ran away.

Hack slumped onto the deck, shaking. Saliva dribbled from the corner of his mouth and he stared, with hollow eyes, out to sea. Cole did not move from his side.

"HACK!" shouted a sailor when he came upon him. "Hack?" he said again but the old sailor's mind was far, far away. The sailor ran for Captain Pigalli. "Something's wrong with Hack."

∾ Jolly Roger ∾

Hack's mind drifted like dandelion seeds bobbing hither and yon on the wind. "Lock him in the storage hold for his own protection," ordered Captain Pigalli, "Hack's sailing days are over but he deserves a safe return home."

One morning, a few days later, Cole sat outside the storage room door and whined.

"You want to visit Hack?" Tobin asked as he unlocked the door. Cole wagged his tail and trotted inside. He pushed his nose into the old man's side. Slowly, with short jerky movements Hack patted the dog's head. From the doorway,

Tobin watched, sighed, then quietly turned and stepped out of the room. He locked the door and headed to the upper deck.

"Two masts on the horizon! Nor'nor'east!" hollered the seaman from the crow's nest.

"Can you see their colors?" replied the Captain.

"No!"

"They're much smaller than us," Yubi said with hope in his heart.

"Smaller and more maneuverable . . . perfect sloops for pirates. AROUND FULL SAIL! ALL MEN ON DECK! LOAD THE MUSKETS AND CANNONS! CAN YOU SEE HER COLORS YET?"

"No . . . no . . . ye . . . yes . . . Jolly Roger . . . both of them!"

Yubi's legs wobbled like wet noodles as he ran to the men loading the muskets and cannons. He grabbed a musket and drew a cartridge from the box. For a brief moment, he hesitated, trying to remember everything the master gunner had taught him. His fingers trembled as he ripped off the paper end of the cartridge. He glanced at the sailor beside him then he pulled the dogshead back to half cock and poured a small pinch of gunpowder from the cartridge into the priming pan. He closed the frizzen so that the powder was trapped. Then he dropped the butt of the musket down and poured the rest of the powder from the cartridge, followed by the ball and paper. He drew the ramrod from below the barrel and rammed down the cartridge, bullet and powder to the bottom with two quick strokes. He handed the loaded gun to a musketeer. As he reached for another, he peered over the portside and saw one of the pirate ships was closing in on them and the second was coming up fast on the starboard.

"Their cannons are small," exclaimed Yubi.

"Big enough to cripple us," replied a terrified sailor who was as white as a ghost. "They want our cargo — not our ship at the bottom of the sea."

"Will they slaughter us?"

"No . . . but they might as well for if you don't join 'em, they'll set you adrift."

"Take your positions!" Captain Pigalli commanded the musketeers. "READY! FIRE!"

Suddenly an enormous blast knocked young sailors off their feet and the older ones reeling. A return volley from the pirate ship whistled overhead, followed by painful screaming as men fell under the attack.

"Hold your line!" yelled Tobin to the cannon master.

The cannons discharged again, shaking the ship in an already boiling sea of cannon fire. The boom suddenly shattered and the yardarm crashed onto the deck. Yubi stumbled backwards, and watched in horror as the sailor who stood beside him was crushed under its weight. Flames flared and someone yelled, "She's burning!" Men dashed every which way, yelling, "Douse the fire!"

Yubi heard the thud of a grappling hook hit against the side of the *GOLDEN EEL*, then another and another.

"TAKE ARMS!" Captain Pigalli yelled as muskets sounded. Gunshot whizzed overhead. Yubi fell to his knees. His eyes scanned the deck. At the far end, flat on his back and not moving, was Captain Pigalli. Yubi half ran and half crawled towards him. The older man was, by then, moaning and bleeding badly. "No, no!" Yubi cried. Tears streamed down his face as he comforted his old friend. Pigalli struggled and with the last breath of life he murmured, "Take my looking glass." Then his body went limp. Yubi cradled Pigalli's head in his arms as he gently removed the looking glass from around his neck and placed it on his own.

When the sailors realized that their captain had been fatally wounded, they put down their muskets, pistols and cutlasses. Many clutched their injuries, groaning. They hung their heads in the eerie hush that shrouded the ship and, except for timbers creaking and sails luffing, not a sound, not a voice could be heard until Tobin called out, "Look smart, lads . . . we're not riff-raff!"

The pirates tugged on the ropes of the grappling hooks and their sloops drew alongside the *GOLDEN EEL*.

Yubi dashed towards the open hatch of the lower deck. He scrambled down the steps. The blast to the boom had blown out walls and doors hung from broken hinges. He crawled over and under the debris towards the storage locker and hid.

∾ Set Adrift ∾

Hack had grabbed Cole and leaned over him. He rocked back and forth with the dog in his arms, like a mother comforting a baby. He hummed in the dog's ear to soften the deafening vibrations of the splitting timbers. When the second shattering blow occurred, Cole tore out of his arms and scratched the door, whining and barking. By the third volley, the dog was frantic. He rushed back to the man, trembling. "I'll keep you safe, me old dog," the old sailor whispered.

The mainmast splintered and fell onto the deck so violently it seemed the *GOLDEN EEL*'s knees had been taken out from under her. Weaker walls crumbled under the pressure. One timber exploded and struck Hack, smashing his skull. He rolled to the floor with the dog still in his arms and the remaining cabin wall fell on top.

On the main deck, the pirates and their captain, Captain Blackjack, boarded the *GOLDEN EEL*. Blackjack was a huge man who easily towered over all his followers. He was laden with pistols and his face was hidden behind a wild beard and bushy, long hair. Slow-match smoldered under his hat and formed smoke rings around his head.

"The smoke of Satan!" stammered the cook.

"Whose to join us?" bellowed Blackjack, "There'll be less work, more gold and better rum if ye' do."

Without hesitating, the wart-faced sailor stepped forward. "I'd be proud to join ya."

Fearing the consequences if they didn't, the others followed his lead, except for Tobin and the cook.

Blackjack roared, "You two, not willin' to sell yourselves to the devil? Well then, guess whose neck we're gonna' stretch first?"

42

Tobin remained steadfast but the poor cook shook and sweat beads poured from his forehead.

Blackjack's forefinger summoned the cook to move forward. Two pirates gathered a length of rope. The cook's knees wobbled so badly, he began to fall. Tobin grabbed him by his shirt. He said to Blackjack, in a strong, commanding tone, "You'd do better to take the cook hostage for you'll not get a better one from any other ship."

Blackjack's face contorted slightly, his left eye twitched. He seldom had orders directed at him. "Do we need a cook?" he said, looking over his shoulder.

"Yeah, cook's taken a bullet," responded a pirate from behind him.

For a split second, Blackjack's lips pursed then he shrugged. "Well, it's your lucky day. We need a cook and we need YOU too." He looked straight at Tobin.

"I refuse."

Blackjack's beard bristled. "You'll not refuse, unless you want to see a man dance the hempen jig."

Tobin glowered. "You give me no choice, for I'll not let another man's life be taken on my account."

Blackjack's lips curled into a cruel smile. "Clear the debris, throw the dead overboard. Seize the booty."

In an instant the looters were hauling away the cochineal and anything else they fancied. After a time, Blackjack ordered, "Unhook the grappling lines, full sail, nor'nor'west!"

The *GOLDEN EEL* was set adrift.

∾ Doomed Galleon ∾

Yubi crept from his hiding place when the only sound that could be heard was the sea splashing against the sides of the *GOLDEN EEL* or an occasional flap of the rigging. He shivered even though he was sweating. He lit the oil lamps, then pulled and pushed the wood boards.

Hack's body lay motionless, face down. Beneath him was the dog, unable to move. Yubi carefully rolled Hack's body to the side and uncurled his arm from around Cole's neck. The dog stood, sniffed the poor old mariner and nudged his nose into the side of his face.

Yubi blinked back tears as he kneeled beside Cole. "He protected you from the falling timber."

The night was seemingly endless and by daybreak the wind had whipped the waters and threatened, like an outburst of temper, to be nasty. Dark clouds bunched overhead. Yubi and Cole huddled on the deck as the *GOLDEN EEL* reeled and bobbed in the worsening storm. The wind increased to such severity that huge wet drops blew sideways and a grey wall of water lashed the galleon. Yubi grabbed a rope and tied it around the dog and himself for the ship rolled wildly as it bravely bore the beating. Ear-splitting creaks and groans raged from the timbers. The howling wind spun the ship clockwise with such force Yubi became disoriented. His only hold on reality was hugging his dog tightly as they crouched in a corner. The storm blew for hours. Eventually the two of them were lulled into a restless drowsiness and both fell asleep. After some time the sea became tranquil, stars filled the perfect night sky and the *GOLDEN EEL* lay in peace. Yubi untied the rope, lit the oil lamp again and wearily walked around the deck, stepping over wreckage and objects that the waves had stirred up from the sea. Cole sniffed around and found a dead fish, one of the offerings bequeathed by the storm.

"I wonder what land that is," Yubi said aloud as he stared at the shadowy horizon. At the same time, he became sensitive to the lackadaisical movement of the ship. He stepped quickly towards the railing on the opposite side.

"We've gone aground!"

Cole bounced and barked anxiously as the boy leaned over the bulwarks. "We'll stay on the ship until the tide turns," Yubi said assuredly but his mouth felt dry and the words squeezed in his throat.

Cole jumped up alongside him, settling his front paws on the railing. He pushed his nose between the boy's arm and chest with a beseeching gaze in his eyes. Yubi looked at him. "You're right, we have to DO something." Within minutes Yubi gathered enough pieces of the broken mast and a door and other sections of wood to make a raft. He secured them together with a rope. He attached one end of a longer rope to the raft and the other end he fastened to the railing before he pushed the raft over the side of the *GOLDEN EEL*. It disappeared under the sea, bobbed up and then floated alongside the galleon.

At the same time, Cole pawed at a leather strap jammed under a broken hatch cover.

"What have you got there?" Yubi asked and stooped beside the collie. The dog tugged on the strap as Yubi lifted the corner of the hatch cover, releasing a bag with a metal clasp in the shape of skull and crossbones. "Looks like one of the pirates lost his bag . . . serves him right." He undid the clasp and reached inside. Pushed to the bottom was an old Monmouth cap wrapped around a rusty dagger. Underneath were a flint stone and a key. Yubi looked at the key. He'd never seen one like it before. "I wonder what this key is for." He turned it over a couple of times, wrapped it in the wool hat and then he put it back into the satchel. He lifted the strap of Captain Pigalli's looking glass from around his neck and placed the looking glass in the bag too. Then he closed the clasp.

Suddenly, the *GOLDEN EEL* groaned and creaked and shifted her weight.

"The tide is changing. We have to get off!"

Yubi lifted Cole onto the railing then pulled himself up and swung his legs over. He untied the raft. The ship wavered, her timbers screeched as the force of the tide tugged her from the sandbar. He wrapped his arms around the dog and they dropped over the side into the cool water. They swam to the raft and climbed on. The raft drifted with the tide as the *GOLDEN EEL* gave a final forlorn cry of misery. Her hull jerked sideways, then flipped skyward. Air bubbled from the inside and the doomed galleon flipped upside down and floated slowly away from the sandbar. Yubi sighed and hugged Cole even tighter. Captain Pigalli, Tobin, the other sailors, and now his only home were gone.

ᘒ Tanisha ᘒ

The barren shore seemed lifeless except for the movement of the sun's rays rolling the gray blanket of night away.

"Stay!" Yubi said to the dog.

He stepped off the raft and waded, with the raft in tow, into a small cove. All around, the rocks were covered with mussels. "Look at all the perna perna!" Yubi said hungrily. "We'll cook up a bunch. I'm starved! Come on!" The dog jumped off the raft. Yubi cut the mussels from the boulders. He built a fire pit of small bits of wood and twigs that he ignited by scraping his dagger on the flint stone. He laid the mussels close to the flames and soon they were cooked. They ate until their bellies bulged. Later, Yubi untied the rope from the raft and stuffed it in his satchel along with everything else.

"I guess it's time to see where we are," he said as he looked toward the top of the sandstone outcrop. In the same instant, from the corner of his eye, he saw something move. Cole did too. The dog bolted, barking furiously at a lone figure backed against the far wall of the cove. It was a young girl. She was thin and willowy, a wisp of a girl with beautiful black skin. She raised her arms as if to shield herself, half covering her face with her hands as Cole ran up to her. Her dark eyes peeked out from between her fingers. Yubi raised his hands shoulder height too; his palms flagging, signaling . . . *you're all right, we won't hurt you.* Cole wagged his tail. For a brief moment they stood and stared then she placed her fingers to her mouth, indicating she wanted food. *Come*, Yubi gestured. She followed him to the fire pit where the remainder of the mussels still sat on the warm rocks. Yubi quickly added more and she ate like a starved animal. The juices dribbled down her chin and dripped from her fingers. When she finished, she collapsed onto a small circle of pebbles, as if the act of eating had sapped her of any remaining energy. Her dark eyes cast downward and flooded with tears.

After a time Yubi asked, "Where is your home?"

"No home," she whispered.

"Where do you come from?"

"Far away."

"How . . . how . . . did you get here?"

"I ran away."

Yubi looked questioningly at the girl.

"From slave merchants," she said.

"You're a slave?"

"Yes, but I wasn't born a slave. One day, when all my people had gone to tillage in the fields and I was left to mind the goats and chickens, two men came into my village and in a moment seized me. It happened so fast I could not cry out. They covered my mouth and tied my hands and ran off with me. After many days I was traded for some shells." She turned her face away and stared into the distance, dabbing her forehead. "I miss my home. I long to see my mother," she sighed, "One afternoon I heard the overseer say he was going to sell me to a slave ship. I knew I must run away that night if I ever hoped to see my mother again." She took a deep breath and struggled not to cry. "I have been running for many days, with little food and only this small gourd of water.

"What is your name?"

"Tanisha." Her shoulders slumped, surrendering to exhaustion. After a while she asked, "What is your name?"

"Yubi."

"What do you call your dog?"

"Cole."

She smiled sweetly. "He's nice," she mumbled as her sleepy eyes closed.

ꙮ **Argan Tree Goats** ꙮ

"**D**o you know the way to Tangibad?"
Yubi asked the girl, after she woke.
"Yes."

"There is someone in Tangibad who might help us. His name is Abdul-Rahim."

"You must go without me.

"Why?"

"I am a run-away slave. If you are caught with me, you'll be in great danger."

"We won't get caught and Abdul-Rahim can help us . . . can help you . . . to see your mother again."

"There's nothing I want more," she said with a note of hopelessness in her voice.

"Then come. We must try — together."

The following morning they prepared to leave the cove. Yubi pried mussels from the rocks. Tanisha cooked them, carefully turning each one over until it dried and wrinkled like a raisin. Then she wrapped them in seaweed and Yubi placed them in his satchel. They clambered to the rim of the rock wall, each giving Cole a helpful push.

At the top and as far as the eye could see there was an erratic sprinkle of scrub grass and thorny bushes that broke the barren landscape before them. Cole gamboled along, enjoying the new adventure but the sun's heat hammered down relentlessly and it wasn't long before he was panting and slowed his pace. Suddenly he stopped dead in his tracks and sniffed the air.

"What is it, Cole? Oh! Look, Tanisha!" said Yubi, " . . . in the tree . . . *goats?*"

"Yes," laughed the girl. "They *are* goats. It's an Argan tree. The branches are easy to climb and the goats love to eat the leaves and fruit."

Just then, Cole growled when the scrub grass in front of them rustled. Out between the sparse blades peeked a kid goat. The small animal sashayed into the opening but when it realized it was alone, it bleated for its mother. The nanny appeared from the spiky growth, followed by a small, skinny boy whose tongue vibrated softly, "Lalalalala." Cole barked and the hair on his back stood up like porcupine quills. The young herder spun on his heels and raised his staff, which startled the nanny. She and her kid darted away. Quickly, Yubi raised his arms above his head acquiescently and, at the same time, summoned his dog.

Tanisha exclaimed, "Musa!"

Unbelieving, the boy gasped and a small furrow formed between his beautifully arched eyebrows. Hesitantly, as if he could not trust he had heard correctly, he lowered his staff and, at the same time, the corners of his mouth curved upwards into a warm smile. Tanisha moved towards him with outstretched arms and the lad folded into her embrace as naturally as bees fly to sweet nectar. She glanced back over her shoulder. "He's from my village."

The young boy stood, head bent, leaning on Tanisha, as she spoke of the day he had disappeared. "Your mother and father presumed a wild animal had carried you away. They will be so, *so* happy to know you are alive," she said softly.

"It might have been better if an animal had carried me off, for now I am a slave."

After a few moments, Musa turned away from her, "My goats . . . come with me . . . quick!" Cole sprang after the boy and the other two ran to catch up.

The ever-alert herd queen bleated as they approached. Simultaneously goat heads bobbed this way and that. Tails fluttered like butterfly wings and a chorus of bleating sang forth from the branches of the tallest Argan tree. Cole circled the tree, first to the right and then left, crouching, watching. Instinctively, he herded.

"They don't *like* the dog but he'll be a good driver," said the boy. He pulled his gourd from round his neck and offered Tanisha and Yubi a drink of water and then they sat down on the dusty ground and watched Cole run and pause, rhythmically in time with the movement of the goats.

After a while Tanisha said to Musa, "You must come with us, back to our village."

"No."

"Why not?"

"The goats . . ."

"The goats? What about your family?"

"I don't yearn for my family anymore."

"But your family yearns for you."

"I belong here now . . . the goats are my family." He glanced at Tanisha and then he continued, "When I was taken, I had my necklace on."

"Oh . . ." replied the girl sympathetically.

Tanisha glanced at Yubi and said, "When a boy is old enough to hunt, his father makes him a string of beads from the soil of our village. If the young hunter gets lost the beads will help draw him back to his home."

Musa clipped, "I have been lost for a long time. The beads have failed me."

Tanisha didn't know how to respond.

Later, after they shared their mussels and Musa's goat cheese, Musa said, "I have to take the animals to the watering hole. Let's see if your dog can herd them." He rang a small bell and the herd queen jumped from the tree with the others following. They flocked together, skittishly eyeing the dog. Cole instinctively slunk lower and moved cautiously, his front legs leading his body in a smooth forward motion as the herd gathered. The dog eyeballed the queen. Her amber-eyed stare locked into his and she stopped. Then, without warning, she flicked her tail and off she trotted. Cole moved stealthily. He circled to the left, crouching lower and lower until his underbelly touched the ground. He stopped. The queen spun to face him and bleated to her charges. All were frozen in place until Cole slowly raised his haunches, pushed his paws into the sandy soil and took off in the opposite direction. He corralled them with his sheer will and intense focus. The herd queen was spry and crafty. She flashed into the flock, reappearing on the other side, head to head with the dog. She lowered her chin until it butted against her chest and her horns angled toward Cole. In the same instant she heaved herself onto her back legs and came down with all her might against the side of the dog. He yelped and rolled head over heels. The goats gave a group bleat and pranced to the watering hole. Cole shook the dust from his hair but not his resolve.

∾ **The Slavers** ∾

Early the next morning they journeyed to the top of the hill and then down the far side that ended in a narrow gulch.

"I used to come here often but something scared the goats so I stopped," Musa said. "Could have been a wild boar, I suppose, but *something* made them nervous. It'll be better today because of the dog."

They meandered with the herd into the shadowy gorge where, hidden from the scorching sun, were patches of thick, green grass. The goats ate until their bellies bulged and their lips were stained green. The young ones kicked up their heels and butted heads. Cole ran in circles and for a while they forgot that they were far from home. In the afternoon Yubi, Tanisha and Musa sat in the shade and ate their lunch. Yubi said to Musa, "We have to leave tomorrow and we want you to come."

"No," said Musa.

"You need to . . . to be with your family again," Tanisha said.

"Tanisha's right," said Yubi.

Musa's lips trembled. "I . . . I have to stay and look after my goats."

"No you don't," insisted the girl, "Besides, they're not your goats. They belong to the people who made you a slave."

Musa shuddered and kicked at the dirt under his foot. "I won't leave them!"

Tanisha tried repeatedly to convince him to come with them . . . to escape . . . but the boy shook his head and tears filled his eyes. Fraught with sorrow he whimpered, "I am always scared. Only when I am with the goats do I feel unafraid."

Tanisha sighed. She put her arm around him and they sat quietly, side by side. The boy held his emotions tight like a ball of wool. "It's time

to head back to water the goats," he said, changing the subject for fear of unraveling.

Since early morning, Cole had stationed
himself alongside the herd while the animals
wandered. He slipped wolf-like back and forth.
He was cunning and agile and he learned how
to work the drove until it responded to his every move. The ever-alert queen was fully aware
of the dog's maneuvers. Her amber eyes seldom lost sight of him. When he challenged her,
she reared up on her back legs and angled her
horns. He stepped back and gave her space but
he never completely backed away. The dog's
behavior was powered by a strong impulse to
gather the animals together.

"He's good," said Musa.

"Let's see if he can drive them back to the
watering hole," replied Yubi.

"Yeah. He can drive them over the hill."

Yubi signaled *come.*

In an instant the dog began to move the goats.
He worked in harmony with the herd; even the
queen sensed a comfortable union and accepted
Cole's leadership. He pushed the herd towards
the crest of the hill, gathering and fetching with
wide sweeping outruns. Then he circled to the

front, lowered onto his haunches and blocked their movement with an intense gaze.

On the other side of the hill the ground sloped steeply down to the spring that was hidden amongst the Argan trees. The goats were thirsty and grew restless but the dog held them at bay. Finally the herd queen became impatient and rallied for dominance. She rushed the dog but Cole held his place. He nipped her nose. Startled, she jerked backwards and then retreated submissively.

Suddenly, Yubi pointed across the valley, "Look! Over there!"

Three men on horseback were riding into the valley, heading straight for the watering hole.

"Slavers!" gulped Tanisha. She turned to Musa. "Is there some place we can hide?"

"In the gully . . . in the brambles! I made a hiding place."

"Come Cole!" Yubi called urgently.

The herd queen's eyes followed the movement of the dog as he responded to Yubi's command. She circled nervously, uncertain of his actions. Her neck twitched one way and then the other. The other goats became fidgety then suddenly they turned and trotted down the hill.

Yubi, Musa and Tanisha ran in the opposite direction with Cole. They came to the steep cut-away trail that led to the clearing. They could hear the riders talking in the distance.

Quickly they slid on their bottoms, down the dirt slope and skirted the watering hole where the goats were eagerly drinking. The queen was nowhere in sight.

"Look, goats!" said one of the slavers as they rode into the clearing.

"Looks like we'll have a feast tonight," crowed the podgy rider, rubbing his stomach fondly.

"Forget your belly and find the herder," lisped the boss through a gap-toothed mouth. "He'll be worth more than a goat stew!"

One by one, Yubi, Tanisha and Musa slid into the gully. At the bottom was a thick web of brambles. Cautiously, they made their way along the steep gully-wall. One slip into the thorns, below, would be like falling on broken glass. Musa stopped next to a boulder. He peered up and down the ravine and then gestured that they must climb over the massive rock. Just then there was the snuffle of an approaching horse. Cole's ears perked up and he sniffed the air. The ridge of hair on his back stood on end and he began to growl. Yubi grabbed the dog's snout just in the nick of time to stop him barking. Straightaway he picked up Cole and scurried with the others to hide under the overhang. Tanisha covered her mouth with her hand. Musa was like a statue — frozen with fear.

On the ridge above them the boss man gave orders to the other rider. "You go along the gully. I'll go up the hill. We'll meet back at the watering hole. If ya' get him, holler." Then they reined their horses away. The clopping of hooves faded in different directions.

"He'll be coming up the other side of the gully in a few minutes. We've got to get over the boulder," whispered Musa. They scrambled, one by one, up the huge stone, passing Cole to each other. On the opposite side, the gully cut away more sharply making the brier almost touch the wall, which left little room to pass. At the narrowest point, the younger boy stopped and yanked barbed branches aside to reveal a hollowed-out hiding place. They squeezed in and Musa pulled the branches in behind them. It wasn't many minutes later that the horseman trotted along the ridge of the gully. He hollered,

"Come out, herder. You might as well save us and yourself some trouble!"

Later, when darkness covered the valley, the gap-toothed boss howled one last menacing command, "You better come out, herder, if you value your goats!"

Musa buried his face into Cole's side and covered his ears when the goats began to bleat and a great ruckus broke out.

Later, the aroma of goat stew drifted in the air.

"They've killed one of my goats," Musa whimpered.

The next morning the sun rose hot and angry. Warily they crawled out of their spiky lair and crept towards the watering hole. The slavers were gone but a repugnant scene lay before them. All the goats were slain; each lay in a pool of blood.

∾ Becoming Five ∾

Musa could not be consoled. He cried uncontrollably as he gathered his few belongings, tying them inside the one small wool blanket he owned. While he did, Cole pushed his snout into the crease of the boy's arm and whimpered plaintively. By and by, he sensed the dog was nudging him onward and he was grateful. It was time to leave this place and the ugly act of the heartless slavers.

The three young people hiked mechanically, one by one, up the steep slope. Cole bound ahead but the low spirits of the pitiful parade subdued even *his* actions. When they reached the crest of the slope they rested under a tree that cast a patch of dappled shade. Cole explored close by.

"How many days do you think it will take to get to our village?" asked Musa.

"We have no idea," answered Tanisha.

Yubi only half listened as they spoke. He leaned his head back on the cool bark and stared at the ripe fruit dangling on the branches. The crop hung dangerously on thin stems. One gust of wind could easily rip the fruit from the precarious twig, causing it to fall and smash to pieces on the ground below. *We're no different than the fruit,* he thought. His heart ached for his father as he struggled to banish the melancholy that rested in his soul. *Would they get to Tangibad? Would Abdul-Rahim agree to help them?*

Suddenly, Cole began barking earnestly.

"The slavers! Hide!" cried Tanisha.

"They've come back! Run!"

Tanisha and Musa's panic-stricken faces were drained of color.

"No!" responded Yubi to their frantic pleas, "It's something else."

"What?"

"I don't know . . . come on . . . let's find him."

They moved cautiously, darting from tree to tree, their hearts pounding, towards the dog's urgent barking. Cole's ears flickered when they approached but he didn't look at them. He didn't take his eyes off the scrubby bush in front.

"What is it, Cole?"

Tanisha and Musa followed gingerly, stepping in each of Yubi's footprints, for they feared it might be a trap. When they gathered alongside the dog, Yubi leaned toward the bush and whisked the branches aside. To their surprise, cowering under tangled branches was the herd queen! She was covered with nasty scrapes and scratches and her big, sad amber eyes peered over her shoulder. Immediately she recognized Musa and struggled to stand but the space didn't allow it so Musa and Yubi each gripped one back leg and slid her out, belly up. She welcomed the freedom decorously. Musa's delight in finding her alive was contagious and soon the three friends were hugging as the queen and dog kangarooed around each other, vying for supremacy. Later, Yubi picked the dangling fruit for the goat to eat as Musa knelt at her side and squeezed the milk from her engorged udder. They drank the warm, rich liquid, which helped to sooth the gnawing fear in their stomachs and warm their hearts at the same time. Musa poured the remaining milk into a leather bag that hung across his shoulder.

"This will churn into cheese curds as I walk," he said.

"We must keep moving," said Yubi forebodingly. His eyes scanned the landscape as a cold shiver tingled up his spine. The unpleasant presence of danger ran through his veins when he thought of the slavers. Musa and Tanisha gave each other knowing looks of dread.

∽ Queen Nimble ∽

Now they were a group of five; like the five points on a star they were held to-gether but each radiated out, seeking a different destiny. The goat, number five, was the provider of sustenance and, as it turned out, nimbleness.

They trekked in silence for many hours to-wards a sculpted plateau of wind-eroded sand-stone, which separated the valley and the rise of the mountain beyond. The sun had moved into the late afternoon sky by the time they reached the base of the ridge.

They stood at the bottom and stared up. At first sight, it gave Musa the shivers. He said, "Only a goat can climb up there!"

"We must try!"

"Yes," said Tanisha, "We'll be safe for the night up there."

The sand particles of the ridge slipped away under their feet so they got down on their hands and knees. Only the goat's nimble hooves found sure footing. Cole pressed his powerful shoulders into the steep incline but his soft, round paws slid, tempting disaster like an egg rolling across a tabletop. Yubi grabbed for him, which caused them both to tumble. They toppled end over end in a cloud of dust to the bottom. Musa and Tanisha slid down and the goat scampered sure-footed with them.

"Are you hurt?" Tanisha asked.

"No," Yubi said, spitting grit from his mouth.

"The goat is the only one that can get up there," Musa added in a told-you-so tone of voice.

Suddenly Tanisha asked, "Do you still have the rope in your satchel, Yubi?"

"Yes."

"We can tie the rope onto the goat and she can pull Musa to the top. Then he can secure it to something up there and drop it back down to us."

Yubi took the rope out of his satchel and they looped it around the goat's shoulders. Musa held the other end. At first, the goat resisted and pranced nervously but Musa's gentle coaxing soon had her pulling him upwards. After a few moments, he disappeared over the top. When he reappeared he had a big smile on his face and dropped the rope. Tanisha grabbed it and pulled herself up. Then she dangled the rope to Yubi who hitched Cole to it. Tanisha and Musa hauled the dog to the top. Finally, it was Yubi's turn.

"The slavers won't get up here," he said as he recoiled the rope and pushed it into his satchel.

"And tomorrow we'll be in the mountains where it's easier to hide if we need to," said Tanisha.

"How will we know our direction in the mountains?"

"We must always walk east opposite to the movement of the sun," answered Tanisha.

As daylight faded into a smattering of pink ripples on the horizon, they sat side-by-side, high on the ridge, looking back over the flat land and beyond to the Argan-treed landscape. Musa opened the bag of cheese curds. "I've decided to give the goat a name. I will call her 'Queen Nimble'." He handed the cheese curds to the others.

"That's wonderful," laughed Tanisha.

"We wouldn't be up here if it wasn't for her sure-footed feet," added Yubi, "She IS the Queen of Nimbleness."

∾ **The Berbers** ∾

They hiked unruly trails for two days. On the first and second nights, circling their sleeping site, wild beasts shattered the silence. Cole paced back and forth; ready to fend off the brutes. Queen Nimble, sensing Cole was her protector, never left his side.

By chance on the third evening they passed a tribe of Berbers, who invited them to stay in their camp. The leader was an old, wise man with eyes that were as warm as melted chocolate. The Berbers laughed and told stories and shared their fire while a pot of steaming onions and chunks of meat flavored with cumin and exotic spices bubbled over the crackling flames. The Berber children were enchanted with the dog.

"He can find anything," Musa bragged.

Immediately, two of the bigger boys coaxed Queen Nimble into their makeshift tent, while another boy kept Cole's attention on something else. As soon as she was well hidden and they had returned to the fire, Yubi gave Cole the command to find the goat. The dog sniffed in the direction of the tent. The children, laughing and squealing, tried diverting him but he darted around them. It was a great game and they hid other things too, in more and more difficult places. Cole never failed.

After a while, Musa presented the Berbers with a jug of fresh goat's milk, which was poured, with great ceremony, into the stew.

"Have you come from Tangibad?" asked Yubi.

"Yes," they answered, "We trade between Tangibad and the small villages."

"How far is it from here?"

"Only one day."

"Do you know of the blanket factory?"

"A blanket factory . . ." pondered the old leader.

There was a broad discussion until a quiet woman with gold teeth said, "Yes, yes. Remember the factory that wanted beads?" She turned her head shyly to the right and left, beseeching acknowledgment from the others.

"Ah . . . yes, now I remember," the leader said. "We had some beads but not enough."

"She's right," recalled the other Berbers who nodded and agreed that they remembered, even if they hadn't.

"Can you tell me where it is?" Yubi asked.

The gold-toothed lady pushed her index finger into the soil and began to draw a map.

As everyone watched the map-making, the old man whispered to Tanisha, "Be fearful of evil men in Tangibad, for they will assume you and the boy are run-away slaves."

"Thank you for your warning but there is no fear so great that will stop us from trying to return to our village."

He nodded his head knowingly, "I will pray for your safe journey."

Just before they left the next morning, Musa traded goat's milk for bread and meat.

Tanisha smiled at Musa. "Your Queen Nimble provides for us again."

"In more ways than one," announced Musa.

"What do you mean?" asked Yubi.

"See how round her belly has grown. Soon she will have a baby — the first of many, I hope. She will make me a rich man one day."

∾ The Necklace ∾

Yubi pushed the hair off his forehead and looked in the direction of the city. "I'll go into the city alone. With the Berbers' directions, I'll easily find the factory and Abdul-Rahim. You'll be safer here, until I can talk to him."

"Will you be all right . . . alone?" asked Tanisha.

"He'll be fine," said Musa encouragingly. "No one will bother him. They will think he's just a poor herder with his dog."

Yubi forced a smile. Then he said, "If anything goes wrong and I can't get back to you . . . "

Tanisha gazed at young Yubi's face. Warmth filled her heart. "We will wait for three days and three nights. If you don't return by then, we'll come to find you."

"Here," interrupted Musa as he untied his small kit and rummaged inside, "If you need us to come sooner, put this around Cole's neck and send him to us."

"That's your father's necklace."

"Yes . . . it is guiding us to our homes . . ."

There was nothing more to say, for Yubi saw the spiritual certainty in Musa's eyes. He put the necklace in his satchel.

Yubi patted the goat on her knobby head. "Keep my friends safe until I get back." Then he turned and walked away with Cole trotting alongside.

Queen Nimble assumed she was going and dashed forward. Musa grabbed her. She was strong and her dogged stubbornness had him digging his heels into the soil. Tanisha held on to her too until Cole disappeared in the distance. Then the goat bleated forlornly and her long floppy ears sagged.

"We feel the same as you," said Tanisha.

∾ Tangibad ∾

Yubi and Cole entered the city as the hot noonday sun beat down upon their heads. They found their way through a labyrinth of narrow winding streets bordered with small shops opening on the main square and a noisy, bustling market. Cole sniffed the aroma of lamb roasting over an open pit of hot coals and he led Yubi in that direction. They sidled up to the fire just as an elegant, veiled woman stepped alongside. She extended one well-manicured finger from under her loose-flowing garment indicating to the meat-seller the amount of lamb she wanted. Promptly, the merchant flung the sizzling skewer onto a chopping block. Hot grease oozed on to the wood. He chopped with a heavy cleaver and a portion of meat separated from the carcass. He weighed the piece and was ready to wrap it when the woman's finger appeared again. This time her finger wagged sharply and she gave a brisk, dismissive nod of her head. The merchant's brow wrinkled as he retrieved the cleaver. With one chop, he cut away the bone and flipped it toward Cole. Cole's head twisted and his jaw snapped onto the flying bone. The merchant reweighed the meat and smiled weakly as the woman set fewer coins on to his table. Then she toddled away. Her companion, a young boy, quickly picked up the package and ran after her. As soon as they were out of sight, the merchant turned an angry face toward Yubi and waved him away with the swish of his big, greasy hand. Yubi shrugged while Cole, with a mouthful of tasty bone, wagged his tail happily and trotted alongside.

In the center of the market Yubi spotted the veiled woman amongst a small crowd of people. She looked at him so he returned her gaze and gestured with an open palm of his hand towards

Cole who was, by then, munching happily on the bone. She nodded, turned and walked away. Yubi watched her until she disappeared and then he let his curiosity draw him into the swarm of shoppers.

Squatting in the center was a dark-skinned man wearing a grimy orange loincloth. He was skinny, so skinny in fact, that his black hypnotic eyes appeared too big for his body. He blew into a small wooden flute that whined exotic high-pitched notes. As he did he swayed gently from side to side. A lidless basket lay on the ground. Yubi peered, open-eyed, between two people at the odd little man when suddenly his attention was pulled towards the basket. Something moved from within. Fascinated, he stared at the rim of the tightly woven container, hoping to get another glimpse of what lay inside. The creature in the basket popped up and as it did, the crowd gasped.

"A snake . . . a cobra"

"A snake charmer!"

Yubi held onto Cole as the snake appeared again. Up, up its strong body uncoiled from the woven den, moving rhythmically with the flute until the snake charmer stopped playing and laid the musical instrument on the ground.

Then the creature slipped back into its container and the old man pressed a lid onto the basket. The people sighed somewhere between relief and disappointment, and then they cheered. Soon many coins were thrown into the snake charmer's copper cup. After a while he placed his flute and cup into the pocket of his carpet-bag. He stood on beanpole legs, wrapped his arm gingerly about the snake's enclosure and wobbled out through the city gate.

"Come, Cole," said Yubi, "We've got to move on."

Reluctantly the dog left the well-gnawed bone behind and followed Yubi to the opposite end of the market where there was a colorful carpet shop. Yubi asked the carpet dealer, "Is this the way to the blanket factory?"

"Yes, yes . . . RAHIM'S . . . good, good, very good blankets. I get you some," offered the man.

"No thank you, I'm going there myself."

A little further on Yubi spotted the entrance to the factory. His heart felt full of hope. He took a deep breath, straightened his shoulders then rapped on a solid, wood door.

A gnomish looking woman pulled the door open, which made a noise similar to squeaky wagon wheels. When she saw the dog she giggled and flashed a coquettish smile. She waved Yubi inside, hopping slightly to the side, never taking her eyes off the dog. With each hop more giggles erupted from her throat.

"I'd like to see Abdul-Rahim," Yubi asked.

She led him across a beautiful garden. Beside it was an exercise area for horses, where a magnificent Arabian stallion was trotting in circles. His thick mane moved with the tempo of his feet as his long beautiful tail swung like a pendulum. He whinnied and tossed his head forcefully, demanding attention.

Yubi followed the odd little lady into a grand room filled with ornate furnishings and colorful rugs overlapping in the middle of a marble floor. An arched opening onto a terrace was adorned with palms and flowers. She beckoned him to sit on the divan next to the open window draped with white curtains that quivered in the warm air. The cleanliness and beauty of the surroundings exaggerated Yubi's current state of grubbiness so he sat down gingerly and encouraged Cole to lie next to his feet. He looked at the animal whose dusty coat was matted like his own unkempt hair and he felt ashamed.

Just then, a handsome, clean-shaven man breezed into the room. He was dressed in a flowing white tunic made of loose fabric that punched forward with each step, exposing tooled-leather riding boots.

"Raj-Rahim," the man said.

"My name is Yubi."

"You are looking for my father, Abdul-Rahim?"

"Yes."

"Why?" the man asked eyeing Yubi's tattered clothes.

Yubi stretched himself as tall as he could. "I . . . I . . . a friend of mine worked in your father's factory a long time ago."

"If it's work you're after, you'll have to come back the day after tomorrow and speak to the factory manager. My maid should have told you."

He turned to leave.

"No, no it's not work I'm after. Please let me tell you about my friend. His name is Tobin."

The man's top lip twitched slightly as he turned to face the boy, "And what do *you* know of Tobin?"

"Tobin is my friend."

Yubi talked about Tobin and the adventures they shared and how Tobin said he would find a friend in Abdul-Rahim, if ever he needed one. Then he told him about the pirate ship.

When he was finished Raj said, "I was a young child when Tobin worked here so I cannot judge if what you have told me is believable. We will speak to my father."

He led Yubi across the garden and beyond a fountain to a little bungalow trellised with flowering vines. Inside an old man lounged on a daybed.

"Father," the younger man said as they entered the room, "This lad, whose name is Yubi, claims to know Tobin."

"He does?"

The old man glanced at Yubi.

"I do."

Yubi cleared his throat. He felt uncomfortable and, at first, disbelieved as he spoke about Tobin, the *GOLDEN EEL* and his search for his father. His mouth was dry as he said, "Your last words to Tobin were;

Separated,
But not apart,
Carried, forever,
In each other's heart'. "

The old man's demeanor brightened slightly.

Quickly Yubi added, "Tobin also taught me macramé knots that he learned from you."

"Show me," said Abdul.

Raj gestured to the maid who dashed away and quickly returned with some rope and beads.

Yubi looped the rope, entwining the beads into beautiful macramé knots.

"There is a special knot," he said.

Raj cut in, "No one outside our family knows the special knot."

The older man raised his hand toward Raj. "That's not completely true, my son," he said, "I showed Tobin for he was like a brother to me."

Raj glowered.

Abdul turned to Yubi and said, "If Tobin taught it to you, he would have had good reason."

Yubi knotted the rope perfectly.

"Now I know for sure that Tobin has sent you."

Abdul leaned back, resting his head on a huge pillow. "Sit here and tell me again all about my dear friend and how we can help you find him and your father."

Yubi sat down with Cole at his side and repeated the story. Raj turned on his heel and left the room.

～ The Moon's Ray ～

Yubi woke in the middle of the night feeling troubled. He stretched between the cool, silky sheets, and rolled, restlessly, from side to side. He felt prickly. Even the cleanliness of his body and the softness of Cole's untangled, washed hair did not soothe his nerves.

Earlier that evening, Raj had waited for him outside Abdul's house. He said, "I must obey my father's wish to assist you."

"Thank-you."

"Ships, good and bad, come into Tangibad. With enough gold, *someone* will reveal which ship your father and Tobin are on . . . IF, in fact, they are still alive. We will go to the dock tomorrow with gold jingling in our pockets."

"There is something I must do first," said Yubi.

"What?"

Yubi explained about Tanisha and Musa.

Raj immediately stiffened and spoke impatiently. "Erase them from your mind. They're slaves! They must be returned to their rightful owners."

"But they are my friends."

"Forget them."

"I can't do that."

"If you wish my help or my father's you will reveal where they are hiding so that they can be returned to their owners."

Raj's demand echoed, over and over, in Yubi's mind as he kicked his feet from the bed-covers and swung his legs over the side. Close by, a white moonbeam cast its brilliance on the marble floor in the shape that was like a square standing on one of its corners. Absent minded-ly, Yubi slid his foot into the sharp, white beam, which was so intense his foot vanished from sight. For a moment he played with the moon-beam, swinging his foot in and out, appearing and disappearing. Cole stirred from sleep, stood and walked towards him. Momentarily, he vanished too as he passed through the glistening ray of light.

Gradually the moonbeam slid across the room and out the window. Yubi felt empty. He stared at the darkened floor, lost in thought. *To find his father and Tobin must he vanish Tanisha and Musa?*

∾ Hunchback Beast ∾

Quietly, Yubi tiptoed from his bedroom. He moved furtively, almost without breathing. On his back was his satchel stuffed with his shoes and other things and on the top he carried Cole so that the dog's nails did not tap on the marble floor. He crossed towards the patio. Suddenly, a hyena-like screech erupted from the dark and the gnomish little woman hollered, "There's a monster in the house!"

Yubi shot outside, crossed the yard and ducked behind the fountain. Immediately house torches were set ablaze and the servants began to search in the garden. From behind, a hand tugged Yubi's shoulder. "Come with me!" a voice whispered. Yubi turned. It was Abdul. Yubi followed him into the bungalow. "Wait here. I'll settle the problem," the older man said.

Yubi slid Cole off the back of his satchel and they sat quietly, listening to the voices outside. The gnomish maid was still hollering at the top of her high-pitched voice, "I saw a hunchback devil! A huge hunchback beast!" Yubi could not hear clearly all that was said between Abdul and his son but soon the maid stopped ranting and the house calmed down and Abdul came back inside. He said, "I convinced Raj that our silly maid was imagining things — not unusual for her. Now . . . what are you *doing*?"

"I'm sorry about this . . . but I have to leave."

"Why?"

"I can't do what Raj asks of me."

Yubi looked into Abdul's soft, kind eyes. He regretted he was turning his back on the acts of kindness the old man had shown him.

He told him about the conversation he had with Raj.

"My son doesn't want trouble. The slavers are a rough lot. If they found out Raj had concealed information about some runaways, they'd make trouble for him and for our factory."

Abdul walked across the room and reached inside his desk drawer. He wrote a message on a paper.

"There is a woman . . . Soussana . . . she can help you."

He handed Yubi the paper. "Give her this." Then he reached into another drawer and pulled out a small leather bag. "Here is some gold to help you on your journey."

"I . . . I can't take that."

"Believe me when I tell you, I am a very rich man with more gold than I need. My pleasure will be that this gold will serve you well and re-unite you with your father and my old friend Tobin. Now accept it . . . you must find your way to Soussana before sunrise, before Raj knows you are gone. He does not forgive easily."

"Thank you. Thank you for everything," said Yubi as he hugged the man. Then he pulled his shoes from his satchel and put them on before he tucked the gold safely inside. He followed Abdul to a small gate hidden in the back corner of the factory.

"Walk that way," Abdul said as he raised his arm shoulder-height and pointed across the barren land. "Take this small torch to light your way. In about an hour you will come to a garden wall with a gate of dark purple. That is Soussana's."

Abdul unlocked the door and pushed it open just enough for Yubi and Cole to step out and then quickly shut it behind them. Yubi felt a chill creep up his spine as he walked into the unknown.

❦ **Soussana** ❦

In the dim light of the torch, the purple gate looked like a spooky hole in an otherwise colorless wall. Yubi glanced nervously right and left over each shoulder as he raised his knuckles to the door. Before the first rap, a voice from inside said, "What do you want?"

"I . . . I have a letter for Soussana from Abdul-Rahim."

The gate squeaked open. Standing in the shadows was a tall woman, no longer young, but stunning and vital. Yubi handed her the letter. Then she signaled for him to follow her as the gate clanked shut behind them. Her dress was purple like the door and small bells attached to the sash around her waist tingled softly when her hips swayed. She was barefoot and her wild hair looked like monkey tails cascading down her back. Yubi and Cole followed her along a pathway illuminated with tallow candles that burned in holes scooped in the sand. She didn't speak but went directly to the stove where she made Moroccan tea in copper cups. Once that was done, she opened Abdul's letter. Her mouth formed each word as she read. Yubi noticed her ruby-colored lips, which glistened like ripe cherries. He couldn't stop staring and when she looked up at him, he felt awkward.

"You are the boy from the market," she announced.

"You're the lady under the veil?"

"Yes," she laughed, "The dishonest butcher didn't like it when I told him to give your dog the amount he tried to cheat me."

"My dog would say thank you, if he could. I'm Yubi and this is Cole."

She nodded. "I am Soussana."

Her eyes drifted once again across Abdul's letter and she said, "Abdul's son believes I am a witch and that I have cast a magic spell on his father. I suppose, in a way, he is correct. The love Abdul and I feel for each other *is* magic. Raj resents this. If I am to help you, you must promise to never reveal who sent you here."

"Abdul has been very kind to me," replied Yubi, "I don't want to cause problems for him or you. I promise I will never tell a soul."

"Good . . . now how can I help you?"

Yubi told her what happened. "My heart is torn in two. I can't abandon Tanisha and Musa . . . I can't abandon the search for my father.

Soussana's violet eyes narrowed under a wrinkled brow. "You feel torn because you know in your heart you must not cast anyone aside. Bring Tanisha and Musa here where they will be safe and then we can make a plan."

"Yes, of course, if you don't mind. Cole and I can leave in the morning and be back with them by night."

The dog stirred and wagged his tail.

"It may be too dangerous. Raj may send word to the slavers to watch for you."

"Would he?"

"Yes," replied Soussana, "He has an unforgiving heart when he feels he has been betrayed."

"Then Cole can go on his own."

Yubi reached into his satchel and drew out Musa's beads. "If he wears this necklace Tanisha and Musa will come with him."

Yubi patted the dog.

"Quickly then," Soussana said, "Before the sun is up. Before Raj knows you have left his complex, the dog can be far away from the city."

As Yubi slipped the necklace around the collie's neck, Soussana chanted a blessing of safe travel.

"Find Tanisha, find Musa," Yubi said as he unlocked the purple garden gate and Cole charged out at full speed. He would be well beyond the city before the sliver of sun on the horizon blossomed into a hot yellow globe.

∽ No Place to Run ∽

The dog was poetry on four legs. His long sleek body stretched to its full length and he paced with a steady cadence. His chest heaved rhythmically in time with his two-beat gait. Head up, he thrust his face forward.

The goat was the first to be aware of Cole approaching and she bleated loudly. Then she skipped tumultuously. Her back legs kicked to each side and her cloven hooves clicked like a Cossack dancer.

"Cole!" chimed Tanisha and Musa as they ran towards the dog. He flopped at their feet, panting heavily.

"He needs a drink!" the boy exclaimed as his eyes scanned the horizon for Yubi. Tanisha looked too, with hope in her heart. At the same time, she filled a bowl with the last of the milk and placed it in front of the weary dog. As she leaned over she noticed the necklace buried in his thick hair.

"The necklace!"

Musa kneeled alongside her. His hands stroked Cole affectionately. He slipped the beads from his neck. With the necklace in hand, he whispered, "I was wrong not to believe in my father's beads."

Tanisha placed her hand on his shoulder. After a moment she said, "We'll let the dog rest for awhile and then he will guide us to Yubi."

They gathered their things as Cole stretched out. In time, Tanisha said, "Cole, find Yubi."

The dog wagged his tail and headed in the direction from whence he came and Queen Nimble trotted at his side.

The noonday sun was hot and made the distant landscape undulate as waves of heat buoyed up from the earth. Tanisha raised her hand to shield her eyes from the bright sun. Her chin jutted forward and tilted upward.

"What is it?" Musa asked.

"Something . . . can you see?" she questioned anxiously, "Is that . . . are they . . . men on horseback?"

Poor Musa shrank like a wilted vine. "Maybe they won't see us and they'll turn a different direction."

But they both knew that wasn't going to happen . . . the riders were heading straight for them.

"We have to act unafraid," said Tanisha, "We'll say the goat disappeared from the herd earlier in the day and we were told to find her."

"They won't believe us . . . let's run," Musa bawled.

"There's no place to run. Our only chance is to convince them we are returning the goat to our master."

Musa was edgy. He squinted into the sunlight, which silhouetted the riders within its blazing yellow ball. *Tanisha was right . . . there was no place to run!*

Within minutes the riders were upon them. They reined in their mounts vigorously. The horse's hooves stirred a cloud of dust about their legs as their heads heaved sideways. The biggest horse, a speckled roan, rolled his orange-brown eyeball so far to the left that only the white of his eye was visible. He neighed and snorted. Tanisha and Musa stood motionless in the shadow cast by the huge beast and when they looked up, the sunlight beamed into their eyes making the riders appear as nothing more than dark lumps upon their steeds. Without warning, the rider on the roan hurled a net. The flat web of rope circled over Tanisha, settling on the top of her head and shoulders and draping down her arms to her legs and feet. She screamed and attempted to shove it away but it was too heavy to outmaneuver. Musa, panic-stricken, lurched sideways and the second slaver slid off his horse and bound towards him.

"Run Musa, run!" cried Tanisha.

Cole fired forward with all his fangs exposed. He ripped at the dismounted man's leg, knocking him to the ground. The man bellowed and called to his mate. Cole rushed at him again, this time sinking his teeth into his shoulder. The second rider swung off the back of the roan and stepped boldly in the direction of his downed partner, at the same time positioning his foot to kick the dog. Musa charged but the slaver punched him in the stomach and he fell backwards, gasping. The slaver turned his rage on the dog. Tanisha shouted, "Cole!" Just in the nick of time the dog jumped aside and missed the full impact of the slaver's blow. The sweaty-faced slaver lifted his boot once again. He was savage, like a hawk preparing to sink his talons into his prey. Suddenly, from behind, Queen Nimble reared onto her hind legs, lowered her chin into her chest and heaved her horns into the man's side. The force threw the slaver into the air and he landed on his head. He was knocked unconscious. By this time, Tanisha was half out from under the net and Musa pulled off the remainder. Quickly they rolled the net around the unconscious slaver and looped the ends while Cole stood above the other man, baring his teeth every time he moved. Tanisha grabbed the rope that hung from the saddle. They tied the second slaver's hands and feet. Wasting not a moment, Tanisha helped Musa onto the horse. She lifted Queen Nimble and he pulled until the goat was draped across the horse's neck in front of him.

"I've never been on a horse," said the boy as she pushed the reins into his hands.

"Neither have I," she stated bluntly.

Tanisha moved towards the roan. He pranced in circles and stomped the earth. His ears were flat against his head and he snorted but he was no match for the girl's fierce determination. She grabbed his mane and clambered on his back. The roan bucked but Tanisha jammed her heels into his sides, loosened the reins and he bolted forward with Cole in the lead. Musa's horse followed.

∽ Cole to the Rescue ∽

Cole's tongue hung, dripping saliva, from the side of his mouth and his chest heaved with each labored breath. He barely wagged his tail as he walked lamely towards Yubi, who knelt and offered him water.

"Take the horses behind the house," said Soussana to the houseboy, as Musa and Tanisha alighted from the beasts' sweating withers. "There's water and feed for them there." Queen Nimble cavorted in circles, then pranced alongside the animals.

The young people followed Soussana to her house. They sat under the shade cast by the massive grapevine that twisted over their heads. Soussana served fruit and nuts, bread and mint tea.

"Thank you," Tanisha said.

Young Musa's unbelieving eyes peered from under dark lashes at all the food.

"You can eat and rest for a few days and then we will make a plan to return you to your village. You are safe here," Soussana said soothingly, "Now . . . tell us how you got the horses."

Tanisha began, "We wouldn't have the horses or even be here if it wasn't for Cole and Queen Nimble."

Excitedly, Musa added, "They saved us from the slavers. You should have seen Cole rush at the first slaver. He was as fast as a cheetah and the man was down in the blink of an eye. Then Queen Nimble butted the second man who flew through the sky like dust in the wind."

Tanisha filled in the other parts of their frightening adventure. As she did, sleepy Cole stretched and wagged his tail whenever his name was mentioned. After a while Tanisha and Musa fell asleep in their chairs and Soussana tiptoed inside the house. Yubi rested his head on the back of his chair and let his mind wander. It felt good to be cocooned inside the protective walls of Soussana's garden.

❦ Tiziri ❦

The next morning was joyful. The birds twittered sweetly. The soft pink sky still held the full moon on its edge even though the sun peeked over the opposite horizon. The world wakened to the birth of Queen Nimble's baby. Musa was the first to discover the new addition.

"The baby is born!" he hollered as he ran back into Soussana's bungalow. "It's a girl!"

They followed Musa outside and gathered around Queen Nimble and the baby goat.

They giggled as the little white kid attempted her first steps. Even the horses chortled as the small goat toppled first onto her nose and then again onto her rump before she learned to manage all four legs.

Soussana called for the houseboy. "Go to the market. Buy good grain and some Argan fruit." She turned to the others. "Queen Nimble must eat well so she has lots of milk." Then she turned back to the houseboy who stared, enchanted by the baby goat's frolicking. "Are you still here? Go . . . go now and do not speak to anyone of this. When you come back you can make a soft bed for the little goat."

"What will you call her?" asked Tanisha.

"Hmmm," pondered Musa. Then he pointed to the moon that was fading in the early morning light. "Tiziri."

"That's nice," said Tanisha. She turned to Yubi and said, "Tiziri is moonlight."

Just then Tiziri wobbled in a circle and kicked her back legs sideways. She squeaked a small bleat and then nuzzled in for her first drink.

It wasn't long before the houseboy returned with the bag of grain and Argan fruit. He was red faced and sweating. The heavy sack dropped from his shoulder. He sucked in a deep breath of air and said, "In the market some men were gathered together. I over heard them talking."

"About what?" Soussana asked as a worried expression formed on her face.

"The slavers. They were found, tied up. Now they've vowed they will not leave Tangibad without capturing the runaways. Also, I overheard them talking about their missing horses and the dog and goat. They said the dog was as ferocious as a wild beast. And the goat, one of them said, would be boiled into stew the first minute he laid his hands on it. I left in a hurry after that."

"You did well," sighed Soussana as she patted the boy on his shoulder. "Give Queen Nimble some fruit and grain and make a comfortable place for her and Tiziri. Come Tanisha and Musa. Come Yubi. We need to make a plan."

∾ Devil in Disguise ∾

Soussana tucked the small bag of gold that Abdul had given to Yubi under her veiled clothing. She and the houseboy slipped out of the gate. It was almost noon and the sun's rays beamed down on them like hot pokers fresh from a blacksmith's forge.

"Use this gold, if you need to buy information," Yubi had said earlier that morning.

She and the boy walked quickly to the docks. The place was humid and unsavory and she felt unsafe. Even with the houseboy close at her side she was aware of the disapproving glances from the men loading and unloading the ships.

Dreadful smells of rotted fish and remnants of old fruits, vegetables and other items wafted into her nostrils. She tugged on the loose fabric of her veil, pulling it tighter across her nose and she looked at the houseboy, who appeared slightly green in the face. There were a number of galleons moored alongside. She felt her confidence dwindle as each step moved her closer to the vessels yo-yoing on the changing tide.

She did not dare to speak to any of the sailors, so she sent the boy. He was small for his age, skinny and nervous. *Who would take him seriously?*

She watched as he approached a sailor scraping barnacles from the low water mark on one of the ships. The sailor fixed his eyes on the boy as they talked. In a few moments the boy skipped back to her. The corners of his mouth curled into a small grin and he said triumphantly, "The sailor told me he'd heard there was a seaman named Tobin on the third ship from the end of the pier."

"You've done well. You were very brave."

The boy felt pleased with himself.

The third galleon from the end was smaller than the others. Except for being freshly painted, the vessel appeared uncared for, almost as if it was abandoned.

A drunken man, sleeping close by, stirred into consciousness. He slurred, "Don't be fooled by the fresh paint . . . she's the devil in disguise."

"It . . . looks . . . haunted," the boy whispered to her.

"Do you have the courage to go onto it?" asked Soussana.

He hesitated for a moment and bit on his lower lip. Then he said forcefully, "Yes, I can do it." He strode up the gangplank. Soussana waited in the shadows on the pier. Many minutes passed. She paced back and forth, peeking out from behind some crates, desperately seeking a glimpse of the boy. He didn't appear. Dread gripped her heart. She turned her face upwards into the blazing sun, which had moved well past the zenith. The drunken sailor woke, arose and stumbled towards her. "I told ya' she was the devil in disguise." Soussana gasped. *I need help.* Quickly she retraced her steps to her home. She was exhausted and felt faint by the time she got there. Musa, Tanisha and Yubi huddled around her.

"The ship is evil. I shouldn't have let the boy go onto it."

"Don't worry. I'll find him," said Yubi.

Soussana sighed and slowly shook her head. "It is dangerous, Yubi."

Her voice was low and mournful. She laid her hand on Yubi's arm. "You are the only one who might be able to save the boy."

"Which ship is it?"

"It is the third galleon from the end of the pier. It's freshly painted so it is easy to find. Here . . . here's the gold." She placed the small leather bag into the palm of his hand. "You must not draw attention to yourself. Put on some older clothes like the seamen wear. There are some in the back room."

Tanisha ran to find a shirt and vest while Yubi retrieved his satchel. He untied the strings and fumbled inside. "I have a Monmouth cap from the pirate ship. I'll wear it along with the shirt and vest." When he pulled out the cap the key rolled out. He'd forgotten all about it. He put on the cap, the vest and shirt. Then he dropped the key and the bag of gold into the satchel. "Cole can't come with me."

"He'll be safe with us," replied Tanisha.

Yubi's heart skipped a beat when the garden gate closed behind him. Everything had happened so fast his thoughts were still spinning inside his head. He marched along the parched, empty road that led to the seashore. Each step on the well-trodden path puffed dust up to his ankles and he wished for the familiar trot-trot, trot-trot of Cole's two-beat gait beside him. Without Cole he felt more alone than he ever thought possible. He slowed his pace when he got to the docks and moved towards the third ship from the end. Except for the change of color he could swear it was the pirate ship. For a moment he hid behind a stack of tanned hides; their pungent scent wrinkled his nose. Everywhere, along the dock, men were working—loading or unloading, scrubbing or mending sails, but there was no sign of life on the pirate vessel. He took a deep breath, stepped out and marched towards the ship even though his legs wobbled like spider webs waving in the wind. He gripped the rope of the gangplank with an iron fist to help calm himself. A sudden surge in the sea made the galleon sway abruptly and its hull scraped against the pier. The paint peeled off against the rough surface and revealed the ship's original color. It *was* the pirate ship!

When he stepped onto the deck two men jumped in front of him.

"Where do you think you're going?"

"I'm looking for the boy who came on to this ship this morning."

One man flashed his cutlass and gave a beady-eyed stare.

Yubi echoed the look, causing the man to tip back on his heels. He said in a take-command voice "Where's the rest of the crew?"

"They're selfish snakes" said the second sailor, "They've gone ashore and left us on duty."

"And we're missin' all the fun," complained the beady-eyed sailor, "What do ya' want with the boy?"

"He's a runaway. I'll give you some gold for the inconvenience he's caused," swaggered Yubi.

The two men looked at each other.

Yubi grabbed the opportunity to tantalize their greed.

"I can give you enough gold that you can buy all the fun you want and then some."

Their curiosity mushroomed.

"Let's see your gold!"

"Not until you take me to the boy."

"We can sell him to a slaver for a good amount of gold," threatened the sailor.

"Yes, and you'll share the gold with the rest of the crew. I'll take the boy now . . . before the crew returns . . . then all the gold will be yours."

"He's right," said the beady-eyed seaman. Then he turned to his companion and said, "Can you keep your trap shut about this to the other men?"

"Yah . . . for sure!"

"Come on then. We have to get this done before they come back."

Yubi followed them down to the forepeak. It was gloomy and musty with the stale scent of salted meat and clammy bedclothes. His eyes darted in every direction and he wondered where the cochineal stolen from the *GOLDEN EEL* was stored, or had they already profited from the thievery? *Evil pirates* he thought. The memory made him feel ill and he swallowed hard to settle his stomach. At the very end of the forepeak there was an iron-barred cage with a big padlock. Inside the cage sat the boy and an old man. The boy jumped up when he recognized Yubi.

Behind him the old man stirred and twisted his head to look over his boney shoulder. He had bushy hair and a scraggy beard that covered most of his face.

"Get back, boy!" demanded the pirate.

The boy complied and at the same time helped the old man to stand.

"Show us the gold before I unlock it," said the seaman.

"You'll get your gold," said Yubi.

"Hurry up!" barked the second pirate, "We gotta' get him off the ship before the others return or we'll be dead meat."

The beady-eyed sailor grunted as he pulled the key from his pocket. As he slid the key into the keyhole, Yubi looked in disbelief, for he was sure the key was identical to the one in his satchel. By then the old man stood erect alongside the youngster and peered at Yubi. Yubi glanced in his direction and was astonished to see, buried behind the beard and hair were the eyes of his dear friend Tobin. Quickly he turned away, hoping the pirates hadn't noticed his surprised expression. He squeezed his fists as tight as he could to steady his nerves and said, "Why's the old man locked up?"

"The captain don't want him runnin' off while we're in dock. Now, where's the gold?"

Yubi undid the strings on his satchel and reached inside. He felt the bag of gold but that wasn't what he wanted. He wanted the key.

"Hurry up!" said the pirate and at the same time he signaled for the boy to step out. "This better not be a trick." He relocked the padlock.

"No, no, I have it here," said Yubi. He felt his cheeks redden as if they were on fire. *Where is that key?* His hand pushed deeper into the bag. *Where is it?* Just then his fingers touched the key at the very, very bottom. Quickly with his thumb he pushed the key up his sleeve and then wrapped his hand around the sack of gold.

∾ Juggling Gold ∾

"**O**h! Darn!" said Yubi as he pretended to fumble the bag of gold. The coins flipped out, one by one.

The pirates' eyes bulged when the pieces juggled in front of their faces. Before the coins had stopped moving the two sailors were on their knees snatching the loot. Yubi seized the moment to stick his arm between the iron bars and let the key slip from his sleeve into Tobin's hand. He whispered, "I will wait for you on the pier behind the second stack of crates."

Tobin pointed to his feet, "I can't walk. Don't concern yourself with me."

Yubi scowled at his friend and mouthed, "I will NOT leave without you."

Then he turned back to the pirates and haughtily announced, "That's way too much gold to pay for a runaway but I won't risk the return of your captain so you can have it all."

The boy's mouth dropped open. "So much gold!" he mumbled in astonishment.

Yubi yanked on his arm and they turned towards the ladder leading to the upper deck.

The greedy sailors barely acknowledged them leaving as each scrambled to grab more than his share of the booty. Yubi and the boy ran down the gangplank, crossed the pier and ducked behind the crates.

Yubi said, "The man locked up with you is Tobin."

"He is? He didn't tell me his name. What should we do now?"

"You go back to Soussana's and tell her I'm staying until Tobin gets off the galleon.

The boy's brow wrinkled into a worried scowl, "He's locked in there and they don't let him out unless they're at sea."

"I gave him a key."

"You did?"

Yubi nodded. "Can he walk?"

"A little, but not easily. He has sores on his feet."

Yubi mulled over the situation for a moment, "There's only one way . . . tell Soussana to come after dark with one of the horses."

"I will!" called the youngster as he turned on his heel and dashed away.

Yubi sat with his back against the crates, waiting. He wrapped his arms around his shins, pulling his thighs close to his chest and rested his head on his knees so that he could peek around the cargo and watch for Tobin. The shadows on the crates grew longer and longer and he grew restless. *Tobin must get off before the other pirates return.*

Suddenly loud voices erupted from the pirate ship. *Had they caught Tobin escaping?* The two pirates were hollering. Tobin was nowhere to be seen. The beady-eyed sailor stomped down the gangplank behind the other man, accusing him of stealing his gold. His face was beet red and words were spitting out of his mouth. He shoved his mate, who stumbled, lost his balance and tripped over the edge of the pier. Yubi heard him yell, "Help! I can't swim!" Instead of helping his companion, the beady-eyed brute ran away. Yubi jumped up and charged to the edge of the dock. He peered over but the sailor had already disappeared beneath the sea. Quickly, he raised his eyes, checking right and left. The docks were quiet; men had finished their work for the day. Yubi turned his thoughts away from the unsettling incident and charged up the gangplank. He rushed across the deck and to the forepeak.

"Tobin!" he called.

"I couldn't get out . . . they kept crawling around looking for coins."

With lightning speed Yubi grabbed the key from Tobin's outstretched hand and jammed it into the padlock. He wiggled the key back and forth and pushed it in deeper. Suddenly it clunked and the post loosened. The padlock opened. He swung the door and Tobin hobbled out. He looped his arm over Yubi's shoulder to shift weight off his painful feet and they scrambled together to the upper deck. Tobin trembled but did not cry out as they stepped down the gangplank and across the rough surface of the pier. He slumped, exhausted against the huge bundle of hides. Yubi hunched beside him.

"I thought I'd never see you again."

Tobin wrapped his arm over Yubi's shoulder. "I feared the same, lad."

A little while later, they heard the rhythmic clop-clop, clop-clop of horse's hooves.

Yubi whistled softly. The roan's ears flicked and he snorted. Soussana tugged the reins and the animal turned and entered the hiding space between the crates.

"Soussana, this is Tobin. Tobin . . . Soussana."

"Hello," said Soussana.

"Pleased to meet you," stammered Tobin as he looked up at the beautiful woman.

"You take Tobin. He can't walk. Here, let me help you up."

"What about you?" Tobin replied as he clambered onto the horse's back.

"I'm alright."

"It will be dark soon. Will you be able to find your way, Yubi?" asked Soussana.

"Yes . . . you've got to go . . . before the pirates return."

Tobin wanted to resist, but Soussana had already reined the horse away from the hiding spot. Yubi waited a few minutes and listened until the clop-clop, clop-clop faded into the distance. *I must get away from the docks before the pirates return . . .*

Suddenly he heard a rustle. He flattened his back against a crate and froze. And then they passed . . . all ten of them . . . a mother hedgehog and nine baby hoglets.

∾ The Foofaraw ∾

"**T**hey scared the living daylights out of me!" exclaimed Yubi.

"You mean the hedgehogs?" asked Musa.

"Yes," Yubi laughed, "I ran like cannon fire after that. No pirate could have caught me even if he tried."

"Then we thank the hedgehogs for your safe return," said Soussana.

Tanisha insisted Tobin soak his feet in warm water. As he did she shaved his beard and cut his hair. Then she bandaged his feet. Tobin choked with emotion as he expressed his gratitude to all of them. "I am awed by your courage to risk coming aboard Blackjack's ship." Cole sat by his side, wagging his tail the whole time, happy to see his old friend again.

Later, Yubi and Tobin sat outside and talked. Yubi told Tobin how he had met Tanisha and Musa and of their adventures. He spoke of the *GOLDEN EEL* and the terrifying storm. He wept as he recounted the death of Captain Pigalli. "His looking glass means a great deal to me," he said.

The next morning was bright and sunny. More flowers than usual seemed to have blossomed in Soussana's garden.

Tobin announced, "In a couple of days my feet will be much better. I'll get work on the dock."

"What if the pirates see you?" asked Tanisha.

"They won't be here much longer — a couple of days, that's all, and then they'll be on their way to cause more havoc on the seas."

"In the meantime," interrupted Soussana, "I'll go to the market and buy you clothes and shoes." She called to the houseboy. "We'll go into the market now."

When they returned, they were excited to share the news.

"The authorities have arrested Blackjack and his pirates."

"Why?" asked Yubi.

"How?" asked Tobin.

"Blackjack espied a vessel anchored in the harbor. It had been there for a couple of days so he commanded a few of his men to row out after dark and ransack it."

"Sounds like something Blackjack would do," said Tobin.

"How did he get found out?"

"That's the joke. The vessel was a warship and the sailors were practicing their maneuvers when the pirates came aboard."

"Ha ha," laughed Tobin, "Serves them right… I can imagine the shock on their faces."

"The authorities immediately arrested the villains and confiscated Blackjack's ship before he had a chance to get away. Blackjack and his men will be doing hard labor for the dastardly deed and his ship will be sold by the Bristol Bank."

"Sold?" said Yubi wistfully.

"When will it be sold?" asked Tanisha.

"I'm not sure."

Soussana laid out the clothes. There were shirts, trousers and shoes for Tobin, Musa and Yubi and a beautiful dress with a matching veil for Tanisha.

Tanisha's eyes sparkled. "It's lovely," she said, "Thank you."

"You'll look like Moroccans in those clothes," said the houseboy happily.

"Yes, they will," said Soussana.

Tobin pushed his bandaged feet into the new shoes and said, "Nicest shoes these old dogs have ever had on. Thank you, Soussana."

"Thank you," said Musa and Yubi.

Tanisha disappeared into the other room to change.

Just then, Tiziri skipped around the corner of the house kicking up her hooves. In an instant Cole was on his feet preparing to herd her, but her frolicking was unmanageable so he sharpened his pace with quick sudden moves that alarmed Queen Nimble. She rushed over and butted him on the rump. He let out a loud yelp that scared the horses. They galloped around the bungalow with dust flying around their bellies and Soussana hollered, "Keep them away from my flowers!" Eventually the horses tired and meandered back to nibbling on the dry grass. Tiziri seemed disappointed it was all over. She had enjoyed the foofaraw.

∿ Not too Late ∿

"The horses are beautiful," said Musa, "Can you teach us how to ride, Soussana?"

"Of course," she replied. She moved her hands over the roan's massive neck and mane, stroking him with ease. "Your first lesson will be on grooming. Riding will come later."

The afternoon with the horses was glorious. They washed and brushed them and untangled the knots in their manes and tails. At first the powerful roan danced nervously. His big orange-brown eye stared down at Tanisha.

She spoke encouraging words and stroked his muscled body. Slowly the fear in his eyes disappeared and by the time his reddish hair had dried he was listening to her voice.

The other horse was slighter than the roan with longer legs and when she galloped she held her tail high. Her dished face gave her a pixie-like profile, which matched her smart and witty personality. "She shines like jewels," Musa said, "So, I'll call her Jewel.

Soussana showed them how to sit on a horse, keeping their bodies straight and their shoulders square. She taught them how to change the lead when the horse loped or cantered. They practiced every day.

Meanwhile, Tobin had found work on the dock.

One evening he said to Yubi, "I went on board the pirate ship. I took a good look at her now that she's empty. Her hull is good; made of the finest timbers. She's small though, a caravel, but I know she maneuvers well.

"Any word on when she'll be sold?"

Tobin shrugged. "No."

"If we could buy it . . ."

"Put that thought out of your mind, lad."

"I can't stay here forever," Yubi asserted, "I want to find my father. There's only one way for us to leave. That's to have our own ship."

"True enough . . . but it can make you miserable dreaming for the impossible."

A few nights later, an unexpected messenger rapped on the gate.

"Quickly!" Soussana said to Yubi and the others, "Go behind the house and keep the animals still." She felt butterflies in her stomach as she made her way along the garden path that led to the purple entrance.

"Who is there?" she asked.

"Raj-Rahim has sent me with a message."

Soussana swung the door open, "What is it?"

Master Raj requests you come. His father is ill.

Soussana shuddered. "Yes, I'll come right away. Wait one moment."

She ran to tell the others.

Yubi and Tobin gasped. Tanisha asked, "Can we help in any way?"

"No," Soussana said as she dashed away.

Raj was waiting for her near Abdul's bungalow.

"Thank you for coming," he said as she approached. "I am sorry to tell you my father has passed away."

Soussana felt faint.

"Come, sit down."

He guided her to a garden bench and they sat — alongside each other — in silence.

After a while he said, "I need to tell you something. My father . . ." Words stuck in his throat. "He . . . he told me something before he died." With a shaky voice he continued, "Many years ago, probably a few months before I was born, my father met a young sailor who had been abandoned in Tangibad. He was from far away. Without money or means he had little hope of returning to his home. My father offered him a job in our factory so that he could earn money and, maybe someday, be able to return to his family. His name was Tobin. Tobin was a good worker and my father liked him very much and after many weeks he relied on Tobin more and more. Tobin lived in the city not far from the slave market. One morning Tobin bolted into my father's house, as pale as a ghost and sweating all over. In his arms he held a baby. He told my parents that, that morning when he passed the slave market a young mother, hardly more than a girl herself, peered out through an opening. At first, he didn't realize that she was a slave for she was not dark skinned. She had her child in her arms. She pleaded with Tobin to take the child. She begged him. *'Please give my baby a chance to live as a free person.'* He tried to refuse but her desperation was unbearable. At first my father told him he must take the baby back. If the slavers found out, there would be no end of trouble. But my mother saw it differently. She persuaded my father to keep the infant. For many months the baby was kept a secret and they lived with great fear of being found out. Finally, in time, they presented the baby as their naturally born son. This means that I, Raj, am the son of a slave."

∽ Separated ∽

"Raj told me what happened many years ago," Soussana said to Tobin after she returned home. He is humbled by the origins of his own life. He would like to meet you."

"Of course," said Tobin, "But right now my greatest concern is for you, Soussana. If Raj learns you are harboring slaves he may cause trouble. We must get Musa and Tanisha away from here and back to their home."

"You are right, except, I hope not about Raj."

She glanced towards Musa and Tanisha. "What is it, Musa?"

"My goats. What will happen to them?"

"Your goats can stay here, with me. They will be safe and cared for until the day you return for them."

"I fear that day will never come but I am grateful they have a home with you."

During the night, Cole woke. He went out into the garden; alert to every sound. He sniffed the cool air. He jogged quickly round the perimeter of the yard. Movement on the outer side of the garden wall made the hair on his back bristle. He barked loudly and ferociously, waking everyone in the house.

Soussana lit a lantern and lifted it above her head the full length of her arm as she stepped out of the house. Yubi and the others followed her. After they circled the yard she said, "There's nothing we can see tonight. Tomorrow we'll check outside."

In the morning as soon as the sun peeked over the horizon Soussana and the houseboy went out the purple gate and circled the wall. When they returned, she said grimly, "Someone tried to get over the wall last night. I'm afraid it is no longer safe for Musa and Tanisha to be here. The intruders might be working for the slavers. I'll send a message to Raj. He is the only hope we have now."

She went into the house. When she reappeared she said to the houseboy, "Be quick! Do not speak to anyone and only Raj must read this message."

In no time at all, Raj and the houseboy returned on the back of Raj's majestic stallion. The houseboy's hair looked as wild as the stallion's mane. His cheeks were rosy and his smile went from ear to ear. "This horse has shown me how it feels to fly," he said gleefully.

As Raj and the boy slid off his back, the roan and Jewel appeared from behind the house and pranced about with the beautiful stallion.

Raj looked at Tanisha and Musa and then at Tobin. With ease he and Tobin exchanged heartfelt greetings.

Then Soussana said, "There is something you need to know, and then, perhaps, you will find it in your heart to assist us."

Raj listened carefully as they recounted everything that had happened. After a while he said, "I will do everything in my power to help. It's fortunate that Musa and Tanisha have the horses and they have learned to ride. It will be a long and difficult journey to their village. Two of my best riders will come with us. No matter what, we must be away this very night."

As the gate shut and locked behind him the cluster of friends felt the anguish of good-bye weighing down upon them.

"For so long I have longed to return to my village," said Tanisha. "Now that the dream is coming true, I am uncertain for you have become a family to me."

Musa's dark eyes filled with tears. "I don't want to leave. I know we'll never see each other again."

"Always remember," said Tobin,
"Separated,
But not apart,
Carried, forever,
In each other's heart."

"He speaks the truth. You will always be here, with me, as I will be with you," said Soussana, laying her hand on her heart.

Musa nodded.

"Now," said Tobin, "Let's make these few hours as good as we can."

Everyone agreed.

"I'll wash the horses!" said Musa.

"I'll help you!" said the houseboy.

"Tanisha and I will prepare a wonderful meal," said Soussana.

"Yubi can scrub up Cole and I'll do the same for Queen Nimble and Tiziri," said Tobin.

The day passed happily and when the sun moved across the sky and dusk came, Raj arrived with two riders who would protect them on the journey. Their horses were laden with food and supplies.

Musa wept as he rode out the purple gate.

Tanisha turned to Yubi, "Thank you for giving me back my life." Then she reined her horse away and the purple gate closed behind her.

Queen Nimble, with Tiziri at her side, lingered near the locked gate.

Much later, about the time the moon was half finished its nightly cosmic journey, Cole and Queen Nimble waited for the intruders. Behind them Yubi, Soussana, Tobin and the houseboy each had metal pots, bells and other noisemakers in their hands. They listened as the interlopers shimmied up the outside wall, hesitated on the top before they hung from their arms preparing to drop in the inner garden. The instant the thud of their feet sounded, Queen Nimble and Cole bounced forward. Cole growled like a rabid carnivore, while the goat butted their backsides. At the same time, the humans banged the noisemakers. The poor pair of intruders was scared out of their wits. They ran around the garden yelling for help. Finally Soussana went to the purple gate and stood with a lit lantern. The trespassers ran towards the light and hurtled themselves through the open doorway. As they scurried down the trail she hollered, "Don't come back. I'll let the lions out of their cage the next time!"

❦ The Looking Glass ❦

Five days later Raj and his two riders returned. Cole heard the approaching horses and barked to alert everyone as Tobin swung the gate. The men were exhausted. Their faces, burned from the sun and dried from the hot wind, looked gaunt. Soussana hurried into the bungalow to make tea for the weary travelers. Yubi and the houseboy took the reins from their clenched hands and led the horses to the back of the house. They took the saddles off of their dusty, sweaty bodies and immediately the animals rolled onto their backs with their legs waving about, rubbing their itchy skin on the

hard ground. The houseboy brought them water and feed.

"I'll groom the horses while you have tea
with the others," he offered.

"Thank-you."

Yubi skipped into the house and sat alongside Raj who had already stretched out his long
legs to rest upon a bench. He rubbed his weary
thighs.

"I can tell you that Musa and Tanisha are ex-
pert riders after enduring that trip. It was more
difficult than I thought it would be. At times I
wondered if we'd have to turn back but the spir-
it of those young people kept us going — their
determination to go home was so strong I could
feel it as if it was a force of nature. And, every
minute of our harsh ride was forgotten the moment we rode into their village. The joy on their
faces, I will remember forever."

He turned to Tobin. His brow wrinkled. His
voice faltered, "This experience has touched
me deeply. I am reminded of my own mother —
a young slave girl willing to give up her child in
the hope I would grow up to be free. How I wish
I could thank her for her courage." Raj breathed
deeply and straightened his back against the

wicker chair. "I gave Musa and Tanisha some gold coins when I left them and with their horses, they should do well. They are safe with their families now."

He slapped his hands on his thighs and dust puffed from his trousers as he pushed to stand. "Every muscle in my body aches," he laughed, "Come on, men. You deserve some rest." They saddled up and trooped out.

The next morning and every morning after, Tobin left for the docks just as the sun peeked over the horizon and he returned as it slid down the other side of the earth. One evening he announced that a large ship, a carrack, was expected to sail into Tangibad soon. Otherwise he hardly mentioned the events of the day. Soussana and the houseboy resumed their daily jaunts to the market. Yubi helped in the garden but the hours passed slowly and his restlessness mounted. Cole became more and more lethargic.

To make matters worse, Tiziri had become a nuisance. Her appetite for sweet blossoms and sprouts had all but destroyed Soussana's crop and Yubi was forever chasing the little goat out of the garden.

One hot afternoon; so hot the sun could fry eggs, Soussana served lemon water to Yubi and the houseboy in the shade on the patio. Cole was stretched out under the table. All of them felt lazy.

"I'm going inside," Soussana said after awhile, "to take a nap."

Soon after she disappeared, the houseboy was snoozing in his chair too.

Yubi sipped on the cool drink and emptied the contents of his satchel onto the table. He admired Captain Pigalli's looking glass. He placed the strap over his head and let it hang against his chest. This was the way he remembered Captain Pigalli wearing the looking glass and the memory gave him a nice feeling. From behind him, in the direction of the garden, he heard Tiziri bleat. Immediately he stood and looked about. There she was, right in the center, nipping at the rose buds — one by one! He jumped from the patio and dashed towards her. Cole sprang up, barking. The houseboy was jolted from his slumber. Soussana ran out of the house. Yubi darted down the walkway towards the rose bushes intent on saving what remained of Soussana's flowers, when, suddenly, he tripped on one of the stones lining the path. He landed with a thud. Tiziri spun around, surprised, and dashed away.

Yubi hurt all over and for a few seconds he felt dizzy. His lip was bleeding and he'd torn the knee out of his trousers. Cole bounced around in circles.

The houseboy rushed to him. "Are you all right?"

"I think so," he replied shakily. Then he noticed the looking glass. The drawers were extended all the way out and the outer bronze ring had popped off the end. The magnify glass was lying on the ground, smashed to pieces. Yubi wailed. "It's broken!" Cole pounced on him; worried, sniffing and licking.

Soussana and the houseboy kneeled down to pick up the pieces, "We can find someone who will repair it," she said consolingly.

Yubi groaned. He tipped the looking glass on end and gave it a gentle shake. It rattled so he turned it over and thumped the casing with the side of his hand. Straightaway, a thin silk bag fell out. There was stitching along one side of the bag that was loosely knotted on the end. Surprised, Yubi picked it up gingerly, untied the knot and tipped the bag into the palm of his hand.

∽ Lady Luck ∽

"**W**e might be in luck," smiled Tobin triumphantly when he returned from the docks that evening, "I heard that the ship, the carrack, that I was telling you about, might need some deckhands. If Lady Luck's on our side, Yubi, we might get hired."

"Lady Luck's already on our side," replied Yubi.

"What are you saying, lad?"

"Look." Yubi lifted the looking glass from his satchel and extended the drawers. The sack fell out. He untied the end.

"Open your hand."

Tobin reached his hand across the table. He stared in open-mouthed wonder as diamonds rolled onto his palm.

He eyed his friend, and then looked again at his palm full of jewels. "Am I dreaming?" Then he shrugged his shoulders to signify *I don't understand.*

Yubi told him what happened.

"Well, well, well," bellowed Tobin, "Troublesome Tiziri is Lady Luck after all!"

"Yes, she is!" chirped the houseboy.

"We'll need Raj to help with the purchase of the pirate ship — if you agree," said Yubi.

Tobin nodded.

The next morning Raj came to the bungalow. He was amazed to hear the story and when Yubi opened the silk bag Raj's eyes widened at the sight of the gems. "There's enough to buy you two ships!" he exclaimed with a broad smile.

"Take what you think you'll need to purchase the ship. Also, take extra to exchange for gold coins. I want Soussana and her houseboy to have something for all the kindness they have shown us. Oh, one more thing — can you buy the biggest bone from the meat-seller in the market and a bag of the best grain. The animals need a treat too."

Within three days the ship had been purchased and registered with a new name. "She's called the *PIGALLI*," announced Yubi. He looked towards Soussana "It's going to be hard to leave you and your houseboy. I can't thank-you enough for your help but tomorrow Tobin and I will move onto the *PIGALLI*. We've got lots to do to get her seaworthy."

"That's for sure," said Tobin. He patted the houseboy on his shoulder. "Thank-you to you too."

Soussana said, "We'll take your looking glass to the repair shop tomorrow. Once it's done, we'll bring it to the *PIGALLI*."

Yubi hardly slept that night. He was excited and scared too. *Had he learned enough to be a captain?* He tossed and turned. Cole stirred, then stood alongside Yubi's bed. He rested his head on the edge and wagged his tail.

Yubi patted the dog's head. "Tomorrow we'll be safely aboard the *PIGALLI* and in a few days we'll be far away from the cruel slavers."

They left Soussana's before the sun rose the next morning.

Later that morning, Tobin walked down the dock looking for seamen he had befriended. He asked if they'd like to work on the *PIGALLI* and many accepted whole-heartedly. They scraped and painted and cleaned. They opened the hatches to the warm sea breeze that blew fresh air into the holds. Cole made friends with the men, too. His demeanor was bright and bouncy and Yubi said happily, "Cole has found his sea legs again."

"Yep . . . me too," chuckled Tobin, "I'm an old salty and he's an old sea dog."

One evening Yubi said, "I need some advice, Tobin."

"What about?"

"Cargo. What can we trade?"

Tobin frowned, "Like I said, I'm an old salty. I can keep the *PIGALLI* shipshape but I don't know anything about purchasing cargo or how to go about it. I'm sorry, Yubi. I can't help you. Why don't you talk to Raj . . . he'd know about trading."

"That's a great idea, Tobin."

Yubi went to the blanket factory to talk to Raj. When he returned to the ship he said to Tobin,

"I guess we're in the blanket business now. I ordered five thousand blankets."

"I'm proud of you, Yubi," smiled Tobin, "Sounds good . . . everybody needs a blanket to keep himself warm."

A few days after the blankets were delivered, the huge carrack sailed into Tangibad. When she docked, every other boat alongside seemed to shrink next to her great length and width. People came to admire the mighty ship. Yubi and Tobin walked down the dock and joined the crowd. They were awed by the beautifully carved and gilded decorations on her forecastle and aft castle.

While he was standing there Yubi overheard someone say, "Look slavers! I bet they're still after those runaway slaves with the crazed dog and wild goat."

Yubi tugged on Tobin's arm. "We better go," he whispered.

"Right you are."

The slavers walked towards the gangplank of the carrack. On the deck the captain and one other man leaned over the bulwark.

Yubi wondered . . . *is the carved and gilded decoration just a cover up for a dastardly deed — is she a slave ship under all that finery?*

The next morning Yubi didn't want to risk Cole being spotted by the slavers so he locked him below deck before he went up to speak to the men. "We're almost ready to set sail. Those of you who wish to crew on this ship are welcome. The *PIGALLI* will be a fair and honest ship. We'll share the good and the bad, the profit and the loss. However, each man is expected to carry his weight and have truth in his heart."

"Aye, aye Yubi," said one of the sailors.

"I'm in," hollered another.

"Me too . . . but . . . where's Captain Cole today?"

Everyone looked back to see who had spoken. And to their surprise it was Timmy. Timmy was the youngest deckhand of them all and he seldom spoke.

"Good joke, Timmy!" said one of the older sailors.

There was a group laugh.

"You won't be seeing Captain Cole today," smiled Yubi.

Yubi went down below deck with great joy in his heart. Everything about the *PIGALLI* was coming together, even Timmy. Earlier, Yubi wondered if Timmy was too shy for the life of a sailor; maybe too easily pushed around. When one of the sailors had told a tall-tale Timmy made the mistake of telling him a person should never tell a lie. But now, his joke had regained the respect from the other men and Yubi felt relieved. He laid the charts on the chart table. He was studying the winds and currents and water depths when he heard Tobin's voice boom from above, "THEY'LL BE NO SLAVERS ON THIS SHIP!"

Cole began to growl.

Yubi jumped away from the chart table and dashed towards Cole. He placed his hand around Cole's nose to prevent him barking. "Sh . . . sh," he whispered.

"We've been told there's a dog on this ship. How do we know you ain't hidin' runaways too!" hollered one of the slavers.

"There's no runaways on this ship," said Tobin.

One slaver sneered and said dismissively, "Get out of my way . . . I'll ask the others."

He marched straight towards Timmy who trembled as the mean-looking slaver towered over him.

"Is there a dog below on this ship? And, don't be lying, if you know what's good for you!"

The boy shrunk under the booming voice and turned pale.

The sailors froze as Timmy opened his mouth to speak. Tobin tried to interrupt but the second slaver gave him a shove.

The first slaver bellowed at Timmy, "Speak up or I'll have your liver for lunch!"

"There's ... there's ... there's Captain Cole below deck *and that's no lie!*"

Tobin charged forward. "There's your answer ... only the captain! Now, remove yourself from this ship or we'll have *your* livers for lunch!"

ᦟ **But Not Apart** ᦟ

Soussana's houseboy delivered the looking glass to Yubi. It looked better than ever. The bronze was polished so brightly that Yubi could see his reflection in it. It was fitted into a leather case with a special design on the outside. Soussana had hired an artisan to tool roses circling two goats with the inscription *'Remember us'*.

Yubi smiled at the houseboy and said, "How can I not! Now . . . let's see how good it works."

Yubi put the looking glass up to his eye and spied across the water at the carrack. He twisted the drawer on the end to bring the view into

163

focus. He could see the seamen were untying her lines, preparing to sail.

"Would you like to take a look at the beautiful ship while she's casting off?"

The houseboy gripped the glass and leaned it against his eye. He had never looked through one before. "Oh!" he laughed, "Everything is close!" He looked again. "It's amazing! There's a sailor looking back at me and its like he's right in front of me." He raised his arm above his head and waved. The man waved back. "Look," he said as he handed the looking glass to Yubi.

Yubi lifted the glass to his eye and focused on the ship. It had moved quite a distance from the dock.

"Can you see the man?" asked the houseboy.

Yubi searched for the waving man. Suddenly Yubi's arm shot above his head and he waved frantically. "THAT'S MY FATHER!" he yelled.

"WHAT?" said Tobin.

Yubi grabbed onto some rigging and clambered onto the bulwarks, waving and hollering, "Father! Father!"

The crew heard the commotion Yubi was making and gathered around.

On the carrack Yubi's father ran back and forth as other sailors gathered around him too.

Yubi's heart pounded in his chest. He put the looking glass to his eye again and saw, very clearly, the anguished look on the face of his father as the sea pulled them further and further apart. Suddenly, in one movement, his father climbed onto the railing and dove into the water.

Immediately Tobin gave the order, "Man overboard, lower the dinghy!" He turned to Yubi with a sparkle in his eye, "I think I remember someone else who did the very same thing, not that long ago."

The sailors climbed down the rope ladder to the small boat that bobbed in the choppy tide. They rowed in the direction of the swimmer.

Yubi turned to one of the other men and said, "You better get Cole up here so he can meet my father."

That evening the cook prepared a special meal. Raj, Soussana and the houseboy were invited to the celebration. Yubi's father said, "Over a year and a half ago, with a loaded ship and gold coins, I was on my return journey, back to you, Yubi, but we sailed into bad weather and the sea pounded on us for days. Men were washed overboard and eventually the ship was ripped apart and sunk. A few sailors and myself managed to get into the dingy. By luck alone, the carrack found us before we all went mad drinking salt water. The carrack is a sad ship but I stayed on her, hoping one day I'd find a way home.

"Now you are safely at home on the *PIGALLI*," said Soussana.

When it was time for Raj and Soussana and the houseboy to leave, Yubi's parting words were,

"Separated,
But not apart,
Carried, forever,
In each other's heart."

∽ Carried Forever in Each Other's Heart ∽

At dawn the next morning as the tide was going out, Yubi gave the command, "Cast off!"

The *PIGALLI* floated effortlessly away from the dock. She sailed smoothly on the crest of the waves with a newly found perkiness, since she was no longer a pirate ship.

Cole's ears blew to the side of his face as he stood on his hind legs with his front paws on the bulwarks and sniffed into the fresh sea breeze.

"When I felt unsure, Cole was my strength."

His father nodded. "It's good to know he was with you."

"You were always with me too," said Yubi.

"I know," smiled his father, "Forever . . . in each other's heart."

Cole looked into their faces and wagged his tail.

Then Yubi said, "You have to be captain of the *PIGALLI*."

"I will be your navigator."

"But you're my father. You *should* be captain."

"You are a young man now, my son; captain of your own destiny."

"I have so much to learn."

"You'll do well and remember I'll always be here to help."

Yubi could not find words to express his heartfelt feelings so, instead he smiled at his father and said, "Well navigator, where are we going?"

"To the Americas . . . they need blankets there."

END

Made in the USA
Charleston, SC
02 March 2014